I Russian Bride

Also by Mark Katzman

Inon

Along the Way

I Russian Bride

a novel in letters

Mark Katzman

Portions of this novel have appeared in bhag.net and Proetry.

ISBN-13: 978-1460983423
ISBN-10: 1460983424
LCCN: 2011904068

First Edition

This edition is printed on demand by CreateSpace, a subsidiary of Amazon.com.

For Pat Carterette, running with the angels

Things are not as they appear.
Nor are they otherwise.

≈ *Lankavatara Sutra* ≈

Letter 1

[No Subject]   September 21

I glad you answer me. When was on work and at home I all time thought you will write to me or not. And you have.

I am happy to receive your letter.

I too look yours profile and it has liked me and I have solved with you will get acquainted. And me have told that we approach one another. But I think that we should learn it.

I shall tell more about myself.

To me 27 years and name me Ivana. On 17 of November to me 28 years will be executed. It will be already fast. I live in small village Tair. I was not married and not have children.

I live with mum. The father has died on war. I no wish recollect about it.

I work the masseur in local hospital. I have finished college and able to make all kinds massage everyone speak that at me well it turns out.

I no know what to tell to you about myself.

What interests? I love cinema, dances. To not smoke, to not drink alcohol. All that to me needs for life to be had. I do not have beloved and consequently decided to get acquainted with you.

I to you send photo made when walked with the girlfriend on park. I cost about a green wall.

Tell to me what you search in women? Tell to me. I very much would wish to learn it. What character, what appearance? What should she be able to make?

I be glad to receive your letter tomorrow hope you write to me. I shall answer sincerely all your questions and hope that you as well answer mine. I already wait for your letter.

Ivana

Letter 2

[No Subject]   September 22

Today I have come to the Internet of café in hope that you to answer me. I very upset today when not seen your letter.

Probably I have not interested you.

It is very a pity.

Letter 3

[No Subject]   September 23

Hello. I hope that your day is fine also you now feel well.

At me so it is a lot of questions to you but I am afraid that you likely will be frightened if I shall ask all. Yes? Or no? Tell to me.

You are very interesting to me also I wish to learn you better. I wish to know about you everything before we shall meet. When I learn about you all shall be assured of you I would make all that we have met.

I do not hide that I get acquainted for serious relations and I no wish to play in any games.

I shall tell more about myself. I no know whether you can define a figure on a photo. My growth 5 ' 7". Weight nearby 60 kg. A breast, a waist, a hip accordingly--89-63-90.

I would like to know very much about you, about in what you like to be engaged of what you dream? That does not suffice you in your life?

I love cleanliness and the order. I love cooking. It is pleasant to me when people are happy.

I hope that I shall receive many your photos also. You are fast to me them will send? I shall wait for them with impatience.

I wait...

Very much...

Ivana

Letter 4

[No Subject]   September 24

I today worked my hands with massage very much weariness much. And how you? Your mood? I hope that well. My small town Tair to be in Russia approximately 1000 kilometers from Moscow.

I am going to deceive whom!!! I wish to find the love in this world. I hate those people which play on feelings of the person of what to receive money. They bring many sufferings to people. I too am very much sung these swindlers on the Internet. I was spoken about them by my girlfriend. These swindlers can break my heart and damage my soul.

I think when we can learn each other well I shall find way to be together. My hugest desire to find the unique love in this world. In that place where I now live very much it is difficult to find the good guy.

I think that on a way at love cannot to be barrier. The love is the strongest. If we in the further dialogue feel drawn I think I shall find a way to be together. I shall make all for our love and for our meeting.

I wish to learn more about you and today I wish to learn about your family, about your relatives. At you it is a lot of relatives?

I live with mum in one apartment. At us only different rooms. At me to have the grandmother and the grandfather. They live in 50 kilometers from us in small village. My grandmother a name Olga, grandfathers a name Boris.

I earlier often was at the grandmother. I much learned at it. To prepare various dishes, to watch itself. My grandmother was my tutor and brought up me. Mum worked also I much tried to study that all would be good in our family.

I no know why but I cannot meet good the man in the country. I no know why but all the man which normal already married. I no wish to marry man which I do not love. Which is not pleasant to me.

I do not love quarrel, conflicts, loud music. I wish to be with man which will understand which I shall understand. With which to us it will be good also we shall enjoy our happiness.

It is not necessary for me kisses embraces tenderness and passion of the beloved, here much that is necessary for me for happiness.

I send you a photo on which I am at window of a train. It was in this spring when I with my girlfriend went in the city of Kazan. To me very much to like to travel but I have not enough time for this purpose because I work much.

Ivana

Letter 5

[No Subject] September 25

Hello My Friend!

I when went today along the street have not stumbled nearly at sidewalk. I went and thought of what you can be engaged and during the latest moment has noticed that now shall stumble and has stopped. And what today happens in your life?

I no interested in young guys. They not ready to serious attitudes.

I think that to us still early to think about meeting we need to learn well each other. I wish to learn from you about your friends. What can you tell about them? Tell to me more in detail. I very much would like to know about them. How you have got acquainted? How have become friends? Whether for a long time you friends? How many at you friends who always will help you?

I no know why but in my life have developed so there were many girlfriends but it is most than me always supported and one helped with all only. Her name Anna. We are familiar with her for long time and I send you a photo where I with her. How you think she the good person? I shall answer itself this question. Very good devoted friend.

We with her always were together.

When I have told to her that has got acquainted with you she has been surprised. She has asked whence at me it is so much boldness. Also has much asked about you. When I have told she has told that you good the man.

I with impatience every day wait for your photos and letters and I hope that tomorrow when I shall come in the Internet of café I too shall receive your letter and a photo.

I think of you...and you like me...

Ivana

Letter 6

[No Subject]   September 26

Hello My Dear, at all I no know as to tell.

I have woken up today that my cat Vaska purred and it was tightened on my blanket. I told about it? I have found it on to street also has stroked. More he from me did not leave anywhere. Always went for me. And I have taken him home. You love animals? And what you love? Tell to me about the interests.

For example, I love ice cream. Simply I adore him. I like the sea the fresh wind and a rain is pleasant on to street.

I often went before on dances. I have a rest, when I dance, when I float. To me it is good but it would be desirable to enjoy this world together with beloved, for example. As you think? You would like to dance with me? I am assured that you well dance and as can learn to dance me still better. The truth??

I send you a photo on which I sit in park on a shop. To me very much to like to spend time in park. As you think in what place you represent our the first meeting? It is interesting to me where you represent the first meeting.

I for example think that would be fine if we with you could

meet on coast of the river or the sea. Sat at a little table. About us there was a boat on which we have arrived and anybody about us was not. Only we with you. And anybody is more. How you think?

I yesterday went to Anna and we with her spoke about much. She asks me now each time about you. Transfers you the greetings. To me to send the regards for it from you?

I waaaaaaiiitttt yyyoooooouuuuu leeetttttttteeeerrr....

Impatiently,

Ivana

Letter 7

[No Subject]   September 28

Hello My Lovely! Is possible for me to name you "Lovely", no?

You like me and I wish to learn about you more and more. I wish to learn from you about that your work is pleasant to you or not. In what your work consists? That you are engaged?

I work every day to have days off sometimes on Saturday or Sunday. I like my work because after I make massage to people they are happy. And I like it because they are happy. However, then after work fingers hands very much hurt but I have already got used.

You would like that I have made to you massage? And you each section of the body will feel as the world is fine?

Today in the morning I with Vaska went along street park and we have send there. I went and thought of how the life changes. I no know even how to tell how to express the ideas but I think that is fast I can. When I shall be precisely assured.

Of what you think, you? Tell to me what ideas at you when you read my letters? Tell to me. I very much would wish to learn it.

Your gentle and sincere Ivana

Letter 8

[No Subject]   September 29

Forgive that I cannot write more. I now go to the girlfriend's home. She is necessary for helping.

If I to be in time in the Internet of café that I shall answer your letter but I shall try to answer you as soon as possible. At her what that a problem with mum also it is necessary to be with her.

I shall soon come back.

Kiiiisssss…

Ivana

Letter 9

[No Subject]   September 30

I hope that you are not offended on me. I could not come to the Internet of café again because I had to remain with my girlfriend. To its mum it was bad she worried strongly and experienced. And we were together with her and I supported her.

Forgive. I the truth wished to answer your letter but could not make it. I have brought with myself a photo yesterday and I send it today. I hope that you receive it. It is pleasant to you? Tell fairly.

I today slept at the girlfriend at night. When I slept to me the fine dream has dreamed me. You see dreams? When you sleep? What you see in them? Tell to me. I very much wish to know.

I shall tell to you the dream. I bathed in the river and swimming have left on coast. Was warm and I have approached in café and villages under a umbrella what to not burn down on the Sun. And under him you sat. We drank juice talked and you spent me up to the house.

You know from what I has woken up? We kissed and I was pulled to you and have not fallen nearly from a bed.

You love cooking or to eat? I no know whether you tried Russian dishes but I think that they like or will like you when you will try them. I love cooking and to eat. My grandmother has learned me is tasty to prepare and when we shall meet I to prepare you for one such fine dish. I am assured that you will want still. How you think?

I always try to come to the Internet of café and to answer your letter. I know that you wait for my answer. And I hope that you are not strongly offended on me and will be as sincerely to answer me.

Kiiiisss...

Ivana

Letter 10

[No Subject] October 1

I no know whether I shall receive your letter and went with hope that you will write to me. And I am glad to open mail and to receive your letter.

How mood? My girlfriends, mum, the grandmother which today has arrived also my cat to transfer you the greetings and congratulations. I hope that you not against if I shall tell it that you transferred them too greetings and congratulations?

Well? I wish to learn from you about what relations with other girls at you were? About why you left.

That you would like to see in me that in me is pleasant to you. Tell to me. I ask you to not hide from me anything. I no know as to describe that that have occurred to me after our acquaintance. I became happy. I began to feel better. Even my girlfriends and mum have told it.

You have opened for me the new world which I cannot describe. I no know how to tell in my heart occurs that such inexplicable, indescribably.

I shall tell to you about that with whom I was familiar. I was familiar with many guys but only three also them liked me especially. I have left all because one has left to other girl for riches of its father. The second is a lot of saws also wanted only sex. The third as it has appeared has argued that will achieve me. And then itself has admitted it.

Therefore I have solved that never I shall find the happiness in the country and have got acquainted with you and you have appeared absolutely another. And even that us divides many kilometers does not stir to me.

I hope that you not against? And I as hope that you sincere with me. Already I miss and wait for your following letter.

I send you today a photo on which I am in a wood not far from the house to the grandmother and the grandfather. I hope that is pleasant to you.

Yours and only your loving and gentle Ivana

Letter 11

[No Subject] October 2

I have woken up in the street there was a morning and I have woken up with smile because again saw you in the dream that dreamed me.

I so am glad that you sincerely answer me and I wish to talk you seriously. I wish to ask you whether you have secrets? What that you hide from me?

I always sincere with you tell to you everything that you ask hide nothing from you. I understand that you are far and know that if we shall be that to hide or deceive one another that it not so.

We with you do not play game we wish to find the love. I hope that you understand me.

I want that at us with you all would be good. I want that we with you would be happy. You good the man also like me.

But we are familiar more weeks only consequently think we need to communicate also then to think of a meeting.

If you for whom I am born that I all shall make what to be with you.

It not seems to you we with you as two sportsmen we run towards to one another we overcome barrier. Then we become closer we learn one about other more.

And how you think, what will be when we shall meet? I shall wait for your answer.

I send you a photo on which I am at home. I hope what it is pleasant to you or not? I wait for your answers.

I wish to feel your kiss I think that it very sweet.

Yours and only your loving and gentle Ivana

Letter 12

[No Subject] October 3

How has passed your day today? I hope that successfully.

When have received your letter very much was delighted you have written to me. I have woken up with bad mood and thought today all will be bad because even in the street cloudy and coldly.

When has come for work was a lot of work and I am tired. I even have started to think that you will not write to me. Now I have received your letter have felt perfectly. On my face there was a smile and to me it became good.

As though you wanted what your day would begin? Since the morning? Tell to me. I shall tell to you.

I dream of what finest day.

I wish to wake up in embraces of the beloved, cautiously to rise from a bed. Cooking good salad and to make fresh juice then all this to put on a table about a bed and again to lay down in a bed in your embraces. Then I wish to kiss you gently that you would wake up also we could have a bite and enjoy our love easily. And all will be happy for me if it will be such. I shall be the happiest girl in this world.

And how you represent the finest morning? Tell to me.

If you can present before yourself the big silent ocean I am so much kisses send you now they would surround you gave you love and tenderness.

Whatever have shrouded and preserved your day and helped with all.

I send you a photo on which I am lady on kitchen.

Gentle Ivana

Letter 13

[No Subject]   October 5

I no know that with me happen. I seem...I no know how to tell it. I yesterday have come home and thought of us with you. How you? That with you? That you are engaged? What did you eat? Tell to me at you all is good?

I wish to tell to you that was at night. I have left on a balcony looked at stars. Thought of us. Also has laid down to sleep. When I slept to me the dream in which we with you together has dreamed me. You represent?

Also has dreamed morning about which I have told to you. You remember? And all was as I to you told. And still we then have together gone to a bath and enjoyed love.

AND IT WAS FINE!!!!!!!!!!!

I no know how to tell to you that I feel but with me that that occurs. In my heart, inside of me. I have got used to you. I never such had also I never felt so well as when I read your letters.

I shall not approve but it seems to me that I am already enamored in you. At all I no know how it to transfer words.

Mine mum, the grandmother, girlfriends, everyone speak

that I have changed, became quieter harmonious and even began to look better but I cannot explain why and as. And only I know.

It happens because in my life there was you.

I am enamored in you. I no know that else it can be but I am not assured. But I think that soon I shall precisely the nobility.

ENAMORED,

Yours and only your loving and gentle Ivana

Letter 14

[No Subject]   October 6

As your day? I hope that after reception of my letter to you it becomes better. My mum girlfriends and a cat transfer you greetings.

Today on work when I have already stopped to work and all tried to leave more likely. And me all asked where?

I hurry up. I hurried up in the Internet of café to receive more likely your letter.

My darling you do not need to experience that you are more senior than me. That we love the most important each other and this feeling in us is mutual. By the way I read that the family turns out successful only when the man is more senior than the girl.

I did not test such feelings. There is nobody except for you. I think that you very responsible person and only with you I wish to create family. Only as you I can entrust such person the destiny and the life.

I by the way wished to ask you as you concern to what I work as the masseur? You like my trade? Or not? How you think? I not vainly studied to make massage?

I would like to show you all medical massages and not only but I no know whether you will want? You would like to try? You would like to try which massages?

I make massage to mum the grandmother with girlfriends also. And they always remain happy. I think what too it would be pleasant to you?

And you could make massage to me if I have asked you? I would like to feel how your strong caring hands caress my body and I am assured that to me it would become much better if I could feel it.

I send you kisses. When you receive them as you feel yourself? Well? You like they? Or you would like to feel them in a reality? I would like to kiss you on the present. You considered stars in the sky? There it is a lot of them, so much time I wish to kiss you. You agree?

I feel that you become irreplaceable in my life. I understand it now. It is so much all between us has already occurred. We communicate not for long but already you became for me the close person. Yes you are far but I think that soon it will change.

Yours and only your sincere and gentle Ivana

Letter 15

[No Subject] October 7

I think only of you. I miss you and I wish to be with you forever. I think of you constantly. I unpacked your letters and I read in their evening. Last time I wake up with fine mood because I every day wait for your letter and I hope that soon I shall receive.

I wish to be with you. I very much would wish to pass with you on park, on seacoast, to enjoy rising and a decline.

I no know whether completely you understand my letters when I send them and you read them but I understand you. I understand each word. And it is dear to me. All that the most dear is connected with you for me.

You the finest the man in this world.

You likely will ask why? Because I never met such as you. I cannot explain much at all but I know that you such unique.

I wish to learn from you about your secret dreams. What you dream what we with you would be engaged? About where we together can go? What we shall make together?

I send you a photo and hope that she is pleasant to you.

Yesterday when I came back from the Internet of café I thought of us. And I have seen young man and the woman who held one another for a hand. I have thought as it would be good if you too could go now with me together we could sit down on a bench and enjoy our love and caress.

As I want to you in your embraces as I wish to feel your kisses.

I dream of it!!!!!!!!!

Yours and only your loving and gentle Ivana

Letter 16

[No Subject] October 9

I adore your letter. As though I wished to see you embrace and kiss. I want to you more likely.

I wish to learn those that think of me your friends relatives the most close people. I no know how they will concern to me if I shall arrive to you and consequently I want that you to me fairly would tell that they speak about me. I need it. To me not important nobody's opinion only your love but I wish to learn that of me think those people who surround you. Tell to me. I wish to know it.

You perfectly know that mine mum and the grandmother very well to you concern. You too very much like my girlfriends also all of them speak that we are simply obliged to meet you because have found one another on different parts of the world. It is very interesting that I think your relatives. They not against I would be with you? How you think? And you? You would like what I would arrive? Precisely?

I ask you to answer my questions sincerely as you always answered them and as I answer your questions I hope that tomorrow I shall receive your letter with answers.

I no know how it to ask you. I shall tell how I can. If I have arrived, you would be against? And who would not want what we would meet you? I think what to arrive to you but I wish to be completely assured that when I to arrive that you me will meet that I shall not go on city in the unfamiliar country one.

You will not deceive me? The truth? I hope that it so. What for I ask never doubted of you. All will be good.

I wish to be with you. I ask you to answer sincerely these questions on them depends I shall arrive to you or not. There will be we or not.

I LOVE YOU!!!!!!

Yours and only your loving and gentle Ivana

Letter 17

[No Subject] October 10

You no represent. With what impatience I waited for your letter. I waited and thought that you to me will tell. I would dream of that what to receive more likely your letter. I waited for it with impatience. I even have come today much earlier than usually what to receive it.

I wish to learn from you how you represent our meeting? I no know how it will occur but think that it will be at the airport because as I know that it will be necessary to fly by the plane. I never flied but I think that I can and I shall not be afraid.

I on all am ready for the sake of you. And how it will be? How you represent our meeting at the airport?

Here I have left the plane, have gone to an exit and on eyes have met. I cannot present at all that happens. Likely I shall simply leave all things to run to you towards what to feel your kisses your embraces tenderness and caress. Can so? I at all no know. At all I no know as it will be.

There we the first time shall kiss. There first time we shall meet and we can feel one another. You represent? It will be our first meeting. How you think, what will be? Tell to me, I wish to know.

Where we to go? What shall we make? We shall be one? Nobody to us will stir?

I know that it will be fine but I no know as it you imagine. Tell to me. I wish to know it. I wish to be with you only with you forever and nothing is necessary for me except for your love. I miss you. I wish to be with you. I hope that you will write to me soon how you imagine our meeting and will tell that we shall make.

I wait for your letter with impatience and I am burnt with the wish to be with you.

Yours and only your loving and gentle Ivana

Letter 18

[No Subject] October 12

I love you and anybody another only you are necessary for me. I am ready to make all for the sake of that we with you would be happy forever.

I no know how to describe now words on mine eyes of tear of happiness. I wish to cry because now I am precisely assured that you the man with whom I wish to be forever. Only with you and with anybody another. I wish to be in your embraces forever. Only you and only with you. Without you I do not represent the life now.

I think to arrive to you for some months. Tomorrow I shall go to travel agency and all I learn. My darling yesterday I have come to the Internet of café but it has been closed for technical reasons. I have been very upset yesterday by that the Internet of café is closed.

I wish to be in your embraces. I wish to feel your tenderness and caress love passion sweet of your kisses. I no know how to you to describe everything that in my heart now occurs. It is inexplicable.

I love you. I love you all heart and I wish to be with you forever. I LOVE AND I WISH TO BE WITH YOU AND ONLY WITH YOU!!!!!!!!!!! I only yours, yours and nobody's other. My life belongs to you and I shall make all what to be with you. You my life.

I tomorrow shall go in the morning and shall learn all that is possible to make as to us will meet more likely and as soon as I learn all I shall inform you when can arrive. I shall be with you. We shall be together.

WE SHALL BE TOGETHER AND I SHALL ARRIVE TO YOU SOON!!!!!!!!!!!!!!!!!! I shall be with you!!!!!!

Our first meeting at airport which we recently represented becomes a reality. We can embody it. I shall make it. I shall be with you. I shall be in your embraces!!!

You have prepared for hands what to catch me?

I soon shall arrive to you and we shall embody a reality all dreams of which dreamed.

I LOVE YOU AND I ONLY YOURS FOREVER!!!!!!!!!

My heart is overflown by love and passion and is fast when I shall be with you we can enjoy that could meet. I, the truth, shall be with you. I swear. I ask you no search for anybody. I shall arrive also we shall be happy. Anybody and nothing a barrier to us.

I send you a photo that it would make your day happy and you did not think I very far.

OUR LOVE THE FINEST IN THIS WORLD!!!!!!

Yours and only your loving and adoring all heart Ivana

Letter 19

[No Subject] October 13

I no know…I no know how to begin this letter....

Forgive...Forgive me…Forgive the silly girl who swore that will be fast with you. I no know no even tell or write to you I so have badly arrived before you. I cannot arrive. I ask you forgive. On my eyes as well as on yours likely now tears. Tears of that I cannot arrive to you. I did not think that it so is expensive. There was that it very expensively. And I cannot find such money.

Why??? You can explain to me why???......Why so????? Why so occurs? Why in this life all not as would be desirable. I lived, you lived, we did not know one another and were sad without true love but we have found one another, have got acquainted and are ready to a meeting and are assured already almost of our feelings one to another. But now it appears that we cannot meet. We cannot meet only because it is cost very expensively.

Forgive…If I knew that it so expensively I would not speak you it. I do not have such money and even if I shall sell ours with mum the house that I to not receive so much money because it already old.

But I shall try to find a way. And if at me it will turn out I shall necessarily make it. I shall be with you.

I no know how to make it. I understand that you likely are now offended on me and more likely no wish to communicate with me because I have deceived you, have sworn to arrive soon, and itself I cannot.

But I ask you to not leave me because you the best that I to have in the life, in it there is nothing more perfectly you and only for the sake of you I live and I shall live and understand it.

Forgive. I the truth did no know. I am not guilty in it. I no wish to deceive. If I knew how many it cost I at once would tell to you. But I did no know.

I ask you forgive me. I love and wish to be only with you.

Yours and only your loving and gentle Ivana

Letter 20

[No Subject]   October 14

I wish you of good luck in your affairs. I very much hope that at you all will be good. I am glad that you have answered me. I very much waited for your letter and I trusted that you will not leave me one. I could not long without you. To me it became much better. Yesterday I have left from the Internet of café to the girlfriend and I weigh evening to cry. Anna calmed me spoke that it is possible to find a way as we wish to meet. We tried to find such money today but nothing turns out. Nobody can give them to me.

Yesterday to me have told that that I could arrive to you to me it is necessary about 1600 dollars if I shall make all. Have told that it is better to issue through agency which are engaged in such trips.

I went there. To me have told that they will prepare me for interview, will legalize all papers and will explain as how to make. Official registration of papers at them cost 633 dollars. I no know even how to find such money.

I have asked what else is necessary what to arrive to you. To me tickets have told that. BUT their cost depends on the airport. And their price is more than 1000 dollars. You represent?

So I cannot make it. I love you and I wish to be with you but what to make I no know. Can have at you what ideas or plans? You know, how we can be together? Perhaps to have what way?

For me the main thing what to be with you. In your embraces. This all that is necessary for me. Not important where.

How to make it? How?

To me have told I can receive the visa and for grandee the passport in 12-14 days from the date of their payment. To me have told that I can choose the visa to visiting on 3 and on 6 month.

My darling me have told that without these documents to me not how to not arrive to you.

I LOVE YOU !!!!!!!!!

Yours and only your loving and gentle Ivana

Letter 21

[No Subject] October 15

My Lovely Man And My Sun!!!!!!!

My darling. I very glad to read your kind words. I shall do all for our happiness.

I love you.

I very much wish to be near to you. I very much wish to be in embraces of the beloved.

I dream to wake up and fall asleep near to you. I shall feel the happiest girl only when we shall be together.

I thank the god that we have found each other. You have brought sense during my life. My life became more sated when I have met you. You have brought interest during my life. Earlier my life was very boring.

I SHALL MAKE EVERYTHING THAT IN MY FORCES FOR RECEPTION OF OUR DREAM.

I SHALL DO ALL FOR OUR HAPPINESS.

My darling I have no bank account. My gentle prince you so it is far how you can give the help for our meeting here?

Whether I no know probably it!!!

I shall try to learn about it tomorrow. I shall hope that I shall find out it tomorrow.

My darling me have told in travel agency that I can receive necessary documents: the passport and the visa in 12-14 days for this purpose I need to pay 633 dollars.

I hope that at all of us it to turn out and soon be in your gentle embraces!!!!

I shall pray to the god that we would be together. I think that we necessarily shall be together. We are created the friend for the friend.

I require your love.

I madly wish to feel sweet of your lips!!!

I hope that it is fast to be executed!!

Yours and only your loving Ivana

Letter 22

[No Subject] October 16

Your letters help me. Each word in them for me as music. I very much love you my angel. Not who is not necessary to me except for you. You sense of my life. I wish devote to you all life. To be always with you in your gentle embraces. I wish to cover your body with the kisses. I wish to kiss your lips shoulders a breast. I wish to feel taste of your sweet lips.

Why we now not together?

You the finest man in the world. In you only positive qualities. Such as you are not present on the ground more.

My darling today I went to bank and asked about transfers of your help for our meeting. To me have told that with this question it better to me to address in the western union. Me have told that it is one of the best and reliable ways of transfer of the help from one country to another. You heard about the western union?

I tomorrow shall go to travel agency learn more.

I am very glad that you mine.

We make firewood at the grandmother in the autumn. It is

very complex and tiresome work but I very much like to be engaged in it. It reminds an antiquity when people would search for firewood that there was constant fire. What to support the family center.

I very much like to look at fire. Fire as a life, languages of its flame as human life inflames more and more and more. Also what it not when has not died out it is necessary to support.

I live only for the sake of you! You sense of my life. Only you help me to live the ideas.

I feel that you think of me and I become happy.

I very much would want that we now with you were together sat at a fire and from the sky on us the moon would shine. Looked together at fire. I want that you embraced me and looked in my eyes. I represent it as you look at me and in your fine eyes the flame is reflected.

It so is romantic!

I want be with you all life. I hope that what be fast we can together forever.

I send you millions air kisses!!!

With love yours and only yours Ivana

Letter 23

[No Subject] October 17

Hello My Lovely Man And My Sun!!!!!!!

I want to speak with you about much. At me it is a lot of dreams connected with ours with you the general life. It is very interesting to me. You like dreams in which we with you together? You would like that they began a reality?

Who knows your friends or relatives about our meeting? They are pleased?

My mum and my girlfriends we shall be very glad that with you together. That ours lives have met you also we can enjoy this fine feeling soon. They are glad that I have met the person at which to me serious relations and intentions. They very much love you.

I want to be with you. I feel perfectly after have learned you.

I want to be obedient and gentle.

My grandmother asked me that I want to make and that we shall make together. I have told that I want to support in all you to love and enjoy love and she having smiled have told that I really am in love also her this feeling known. She very much would want to test it once again but the grandfather has left also she cannot forget it never.

My darling tomorrow I shall go to travel agency I shall tell that soon we shall start to do necessary documents for our meeting. After tomorrow I descend in bank learn all the exact information on the western union as it works. I shall write tomorrow the information which I learn.

My darling I shall do everything that in my forces for our meeting and for our general happiness. I too very much try to find what or a way for reception of the necessary sum what to pay to travel agency.

I want to be with you want to love you want to enjoy our tenderness want to give love caress to you want care about you feel your love in a reality. I think that you my love I want to be with you forever.

You my destiny!!!!!

I want to hear more your dreams to know that you think also want to kiss you now to be in your gentle embraces. I with impatience wait when it happen.

I love you!

Yours and only your loving Ivana

Letter 24

[No Subject]   October 18

Hello My Lovely Man And My Sun!!!!!!!!

My love of you warms your letters when I receive them.

I ADORE YOU!!!!!!!

My darling I am happy the news that we can soon start to do our documents. I very much wish to appear more likely in your embraces.

My darling I studied English language at school and after in college. I know him not badly but I speak better than I write.

I last night have decided to go on park. I went along the street all over again have then come in park and sat on a bench. In our park it is a lot of bushes a lot of trees lanterns now stand and there it is bright.

I thought of that as it would be fine to go together with you in park. It is a lot of boys and girls which else study at university or parents with children went on park but I noticed only young pairs. They went together held hands together embraced kissed laughed.

You would be desirable that with me now I could embrace you sit to you on knees kiss you gently and passionately?

I want to be with you. I want to feel yours. I want to feel the heat. I want that we groaned with happiness and love.

You are not present with me and to me is sad without you. I believe only in that there will come day happy for us and we with you shall be in embraces of one another. All we shall make together we shall make so our life would be full of happiness and love.

I want to be with you my love. I want to enjoy our happiness and love and would want that we forever were together.

I send you the kisses the most gentle that you could feel my tenderness that your heart would be warmed that your ideas would be about me and you have written to me the big and gentle letter.

I love you!!!!

Yours and only your gentle and sweet Ivana

Letter 25

[No Subject]   October 19

Hello My Lovely Man And My Sun!!!!!!!!

You say, I live to embrace you. I am very grateful to you for letters gentle and full of love. I very much miss you is glad to receive yours the letter. My darling I too very much miss on you. I at night very long can no fall asleep. I think about our meeting much.

Mum speaks that I appear now very happy. I very glad that we fast can be together. My gentle prince I wish to feel more likely your gentle kisses. I dream to be in your embraces.

To me have told that in mine town there is no western union but I have learned that the western union is in the next city. My darling I without problems can receive your help for our meeting there.

Here the address of the western union RUSSIA street ENGELSA 3 city CHEBOKSARY.

My full name and surname Ivana Zemonova. To me have told that this information will be necessary for transfer of the help for our meeting for you only.

Everyone in life has two stripes, black and white, the period of failures is black, white - happiness and love. After I have met you in my life there was only a white stripe.

I feel perfectly because I feel your love. I want to be with you. I want to make love.

I WANT TO LIVE IN THE NAME OF OUR LOVE!!!!

I forever yours and only yours. You for me the closest person. Same close as mum and the grandmother.

You the person which have presented me the most fine feeling and I adore you for it. I want that we always were together that we would be always full of passion that our kisses would warm us each minute.

You so dear to me. I feel that we are created one for another. The destiny has prepared us for test as distance but I hope that we shall overcome it. Everyone in this world has happiness. The main thing to find it. I have found the happiness and the love.

IT YOU!!!!!!!

You forever in my heart.

Your loving and gentle Ivana

Letter 26

[No Subject]   October 20

Hello My Lovely Man And My Sun!!!!!!

I'm fine. Mum asks to transfer you the greetings and congratulations but me it is very boring without you. It is boring because I cannot be with you and enjoy our happiness and love.

I very much want to be with you that we were together. I want to feel your embraces kisses your tenderness and love. I thought of that as it would be good if we could go together to shop choose one to another good things a meal or still that or.

We together take the carriage also shall push it there that it is necessary. You will put the hand on mine and we slowly shall go along a counter. We shall take various foods, spices green fruit bread and many other things that I could prepare for tasty dishes for us and we enjoyed them each day.

My darling I did typing error in my surname. You should alter my surname on ZEMONOVA. I can receive your help only if you again will go to the western union and write now there ZEMANOVA. My darling forgive that I give to you so much efforts.

In shop of clothes we shall buy clothes for you or me. I shall help you to choose the most beautiful suit you will look always fine and you help to me choose a beautiful dress. I cannot choose itself basically I am helped by the girlfriend. I know that you too will help me choose the most beautiful dress in which I shall love you and you will love me in it. You will help me to choose female linen? I would want that it was pleasant to you and I hope that you will not refuse to help me in a choice of it.

I will be sure that our life is fine because we shall make all that it was filled with happiness love and I am very glad that I have you. You for me the most fine most necessary favourite person.

You all world for me I live each day only because I have you and soon our lives begin full bright paints.

You in my heart I madly love you.

Yours and only your loving Ivana

Letter 27

[No Subject] October 21

Hello My Lovely Man And My Sun!!!!!!!!

I very much miss on you. I very much want to be with you. I would want that you were in my embraces and I could sit on yours knees. I frequently think of that as we together are engaged in love.

I many times imagined ours with you the first night of love. I am sure we no shall to sleep this night. We shall enjoy our love that first night I shall not forget never. I know you will make all as well that we would be happy and groaned from love and happiness.

We shall be in a bed and we shall not leave it. Only sometimes to have a drink coffee or to eat a sandwich. We shall accept bathing with you we shall caress one another to help be washed. When I think of it that on my body runs a shiver now I have decided to stop this subject. I cannot write now the big details because very much was excited when the beginnings to think of it. What you think of our first night of love? How you imagine to yourself it?

My darling today I have received your help for our meeting. I am glad that soon we shall be together. My darling today before going to the Internet of café I descended in travel agency have paid for documents which are necessary for our meeting.

My darling thanks you for everything that you do for our love. I very strongly love you my gentle prince. I am happy that we have taken the first step to our meeting. I shall be the happiest girl in the world when I can enjoy your gentle kisses.

My darling learn please the name of city where to be the most close airport to you. I need to know the name of city the name of the airport of what to learn exact cost of air tickets.

I with impatience wait for your letter.

Yours and only your loving Ivana

Letter 28

[No Subject]   October 22

Hello My Lovely Man And My Sun!!!!!!!!!!!

Today at me good day. I have woken up with good mood. Saw fine dream at night. Has received your letter but much does not suffice for full happiness.

I no have not enough your embraces kisses gentle words passion tenderness love. I want to feel your breath but all this only in dreams but I believe that they begin a reality and me to become more easy.

My darling tomorrow I shall go to travel agency and find out exact cost of cheapest tickets up to Atlanta, Georgia. I shall write tomorrow everything I have learned.

I missing on you. I think of you I dream of that as we are engaged in love as we groan of happiness passions and love.

When I went today on street have not come nearly in a hole I thought of you not notice it only before it have suddenly stopped. You would be desirable that with me that I could go together with you and hold you for a hand? Could talk to you about all?

In the evening we could look TV have supper together kiss to caress one another make love.

I want to fill ours with you what did not suffice us while we have not got acquainted. I did not have not enough love tenderness caress and I have found it with you but now I still do not have it more strongly and I no know what to make what we have met faster.

All my ideas only about you about that as it will be good when we can be together. I love you and I know that it not simply words this feeling which lives in my heart helps me to live and knock to my heart which belongs to you!

Yours and only your loving Ivana

Letter 29

[No Subject]   October 23

Hello My Lovely Man And My Sun!!!!!!!!!

I miss you. I think of you is glad your to the letter. What you made today? That was engaged? Of what you think when you sleep? Of what you dream? What you ate? Whether it is tired on work? Where you would want to go? Whether at me so it is a lot of questions to you and I at all do not know time will suffice at you to answer all.

My darling today I went to travel agency and have told it the name of your airport. To me have told it still depends on date of a start more not many. I have told that on November, 5th. To me have told that I would come tomorrow and they will inform me exact cost of the ticket aboard the plane up to Atlanta for November, 5th. My darling I have hurried having told on November, 5th??? Yes? I need to learn for December, 1st? My darling I very much wish to be near to you more likely but if you tell that was not present I shall ask about December, 1st.

I think of you think of us think of ours future. I think of that as life became fine after I have got acquainted with you. For all time of our dialogue to me it was bad only once when I have learned that I cannot arrive to you and we not be together quickly. Yes then I cried from misfortune to me it was very bad. I no know what to write to you then my heart was sick and groaned from a pain.

But now I am happy I think and I dream of you. Dreams help me to live they raise me but it would be desirable to be in your embraces would be desirable to make to you fine supper. It would be desirable to kiss embrace make love talk to you feel your breath tenderness caress.

Though I meet each day and see off without you it seem that you with me. I receive your letters and I glad. Letters help me to live. I think that when we shall be together that we much as we shall recollect that as we have got acquainted have fallen in love and have met. We shall look at ours with you photo and to enjoy them.

I love you send you all the tenderness caress together with kisses and I hope that to you well when you read my letter.

Yours and only your loving Ivana

Letter 30

[No Subject]   October 24

Hello My Lovely Man And My Sun!!!!!!

My love I miss you your letter again brought pleasure and a smile. I adore you!

Today on work all was good and there were no incidents. Only one woman left home. To her would tell that she laid in a bed and sometimes only would not rise what to go in a toilet but she has told that has gone to a toilet and itself has gone to exits and only in the street her have caught up and have returned back. When her have asked what for she has made she of anything has told but has begun to cry. She and nothing speaks only lays on a bed and cries. I calmed her then. It appears her the favourite person has stopped and she waits when he will return. At her the strongest stress a heart attack if her mother has not caused medical care and her have not taken away home. She upset her man does not come any more to her and she wanted to descend wash learn he came whether or not. We long spoke and there was that all happen for that she worked much and not enough time carried out with it and he has told that cannot any more has left. I calmed also have told her that he return. That if the love is true that he cannot without her. She has then fallen asleep and when I left she strong slept.

My darling I very much wish to be more likely in your embraces. I very much wish to feel your kisses. I wish to fly to your embraces more likely.

Today went to travel agency have learned about cost of tickets. To me have told that tickets up to Atlanta on November, 5th will cost 1187 US dollars.

My darling I very much miss on you. Now almost every night the dream dreams me of our meeting. I love you.

I am grateful to destiny we have found each other in this huge world. I will not be sure at us such and we shall carry out a lot of time together and we shall never swear at you. I no like to swear no like to be nervous and shout.

I would want that in ours with you the house there only tenderness love and happiness caress all only the most good. I make all that it would be and I hope that you will help me with it.

I very much love you!!!! I would want that we always were happy. I would want that we always had good mood and we always enjoyed our love. I very much miss you and I want to be with you.

I hope that we can meet soon.

Yours and only your loving Ivana

Letter 31

[No Subject]   October 25

Hello My Lovely Man And My Sun!!!!

I glad to receive your letter. At me at once was cheered up also to me it became very good.

I dream of you my love. I dream about our long passionate nights of love pleasant walks in park in the street on a beach. I dream of that as we shall swim together. As I shall be in your embraces tender gentle as we shall kiss one another as we shall make love.

Yesterday we talked to mum about us with you much. She speaks that she very happy for us with you has told that expresses you the gratitude for that that you have made me so happy.

When I was at the grandmother the grandmother have told to us with you very much has carried because to meet the present love difficultly and very difficultly save it when appear problem. I have told that we with you shall overcome all problems in our life and she has told that knows it. She has told that trusts in our love and transfers you the greetings.

All my girlfriends also wait when can receive a photo where

we with you together. They speak that we with you very want to see happy persons and smiles. As has told Anna she never saw me such happy while I have not met you. I have told that itself never felt like so well.

My darling on second of November my documents will be ready. Yes I asked the visa for 6 months. My darling my visa refers to the tourist visa.

My heart knocks only while our love lives in it. I am sure we shall to live long and would want we forever were together and were never separated.

I love you!

Yours and only your loving Ivana

Letter 32

[No Subject]   October 26

Hello My Lovely Man And My Sun!!!!!!

I am glad to receive your letter today. I have thought up poem and send it to you.

We require love to feel each other,
We require feelings to like each other,
We require in all that makes us closer,
And nothing will separate us, nothing will destroy our love,
Which every day all becomes more strong.

This poem which I have sent you sounds from my soul. I think dream of our meeting our fine travel our love.

I very much miss on you. I see dreams of ours with you the future and they are fine. I want to embody them in a reality. I very much want to be with you. I want to enjoy our happiness and love.

Today we with mum went in shop to buy products. We have bought all necessary sugar groats salt and many other things. Now can some weeks to not go to shop.

What you have made today? You saw dreams? If yes about what?

I dreamt we with you sat in a room in which burned only candles. Pleasant slow music played and we had supper with you. Was so perfectly to sit opposite to you and to see your sight which is gentle and with love looks at me on your smile which bewitches it would be desirable to kiss you. Then an alarm clock all was finished.

Probably today I shall see continuation of this dream. And you can it will see?

About it we learn tomorrow.

Yours and only your loving Ivana

Letter 33

[No Subject]   October 27

Hello My Lovely Man And My Sun!!!!!!!

My darling I tomorrow shall go to a public telephone booth and shall try to call to you.

Today I am very tired on work and still now it is necessary to go to one woman with mum ask to transfer her what that documents. She has left them on work and I shall take them to her home.

It would be good if you have gone with me embrace me the hand that I could feel as your hands caress my body and could kiss you caress you. I think that we long went in this woman. How you think?

I yesterday looked at the sky. It so is fine. On it of a star which it is alone one from another. We with you as they far also cannot meet but they cannot meet never and we meet and is very fast. I dream of day to our meeting. I so many times represented her to myself and all time on miscellaneous. I no know as it will be exact but I will be sure that it is fine.

My mum girlfriends transfer you the greetings. They very much want to look a photo on which we together. We shall give to them such pleasure?

Yours and only yours on all life Ivana

Letter 34

[No Subject]   October 28

Hello My Lovely Man And My Sun!!!!

Today good and clear weather. I very glad to see your letter which warms me better my heart my love which in my blood warms my body. I very much miss you.

Each evening I re-read your letters. I think of you. You always with me. Mine girlfriends constantly ask me about that as you and as your affairs.

Today has met Katya the school girlfriend. She no know about you and has asked as my life. I have told that all well. She has looked and has asked me. Whether she has asked have found the love whether have left in marriage. I have told that in marriage has not left but the love has met. I have told to her about you and she was very much surprised having heard such history. She has told that could not even think about how people can learn one another for thousand kilometers. She married also husband drinks also they prepare to divorce much.

They not are happy because no know such the present love but I know it only due to you. I glad to this feeling and hope that we shall meet enjoy it. I know shall never regret about anything when we shall be together. For me the happiness to be with you want that it became a reality.

We can make all about that dreamed and our love will live always in our hearts. I with impatience wait for your letter. We shall overcome all barrier which us divide we shall be together.

I love you!!!!

Yours and only your loving Ivana

Letter 35

[No Subject]   October 29

Hello My Lovely Man And My Sun!!!!!!!

Your letter as beams of the Sun which shine me warms me makes me happy. You say your lips will be forever touching mine! Your arms surrounding me always!

My darling I tried to find a public telephone booth but in mine town there is no public telephone booth. Public telephone booths only in cities. I think shall call to you from Moscow before the start to you.

Darling my documents will be ready on second of November. When we can pay tickets aboard the plane? I cannot live without you. I cannot feel like normally. Each minute I want to be with you. This especially difficult at night. So it would be desirable to be with you. I live for our nights.

It would be desirable to see as you smile enjoy supper which I prepare. It would be desirable to feel your love. It would be desirable to feel your tenderness.

When I wake up the morning I want to embrace you sit on you make to you massage. I would like to kiss you. To kiss while you wake up and embrace me.

I fall asleep dream that we together. I wake up with ideas that we together. I prepare for supper prepare for breakfast prepare for dinner. I no know as to describe that with me occurs. I simply cannot present the life without you. I no know as I lived earlier.

HOW I COULD LIVE WITHOUT YOU???? To me it would be very bad if you have left me one now but I believe that you will make it. That we soon shall be together.

I love you and wait impatiently for your letter.

Yours and only your loving Ivana

Letter 36

[No Subject]   October 30

Hello My Lovely Man And My Sun!!!!!!!

I miss you. I glad to receive your letter which brings me love and hope.

My darling I no know precisely how many live people in mine town is assured that in mine town Tair we live less than 1000 person.

I would like to be with you more than anything. All my desires and dreams connected only to you. As you have lead today? What you ate? What mood at you?

You saw fine dreams of us with you that we kissed! I saw one dream recently. About that as we with you made photos for our album. BY WHAT ONLY PHOTO WE DID NOT MAKE!!!!!

I want to be with you only with you. I want to enjoy ours love and happiness. I want that we were together.

I love you!!!!! You my heart and my life!

Yours and only your loving Ivana

Letter 37

[No Subject] October 31

Hello My Lovely Sun!!!!!

I no know why but melancholy shrouds me. Likely because I cannot feel your kisses your love your tenderness breath on the present.

Sometimes I wake up in the morning and me seem that you with me but anybody is not present.

The bed is empty. I go to a bath one and I cannot go there together with you. I would not like to use a make-up at all. You do not see me and more I for anybody do not want to be beautiful.

My beauty was seen by you. You have presented me love and I glad to this feeling. I am happy only in dreams now but I believe that they become a reality I believe that we soon shall be together.

I yesterday talked to mum. She asks as you. When we gather I speak that I no know still but I hope that soon. She supports me helps me to wait for our meeting.

If I could be for seconds with you I would give all that at me is.

I have not regretted anything just to touch your lips kiss see your tender sight full of love and tenderness.

But it is impossible. I no know as it to make.

When I sleep at night I want to sleep with you want to feel your heat. I want to talk to you and to hear your voice. When I lie down to sleep that you always with me.

I re-read your letters your dreams and to me it becomes better. Tell to me more about the dreams. They are fine. They very much love to me.

I wait for your letter. I love you!

Yours and only your loving Ivana

Letter 38

[No Subject] November 1

Hello My Lovely Man And My Sun!!!!!!!

My love I glad that you write me and do not overlook about me.

My darling tomorrow my documents will be ready. To me have told that I shall receive them in Moscow in the American embassy.

I hope what be fast we can together. I think of us much. I say to you about that I dream you know all my feelings I cannot tell to you all dreams because them very much. I would not have not enough time what to write them all but glad that I can say you even some.

I yesterday looked at night a film. I could not fall asleep and have included TV on what that the channel at night and looked film. I no know as its name to but it was film about love of tenderness and passion it Russian film. When I looked as actors made love I would dream that also we with you could so.

I want to embrace you kiss you your a body to be engaged with you in love. I want run in one shirt on house that we could enjoy love when we shall want. As soon as at us the desire we one will appear could approach to another excite enjoy passion.

I saw as they made love. As in their eyes burned passion fire love as she shuddered when all came to an end as they happy woke up in the morning.

I would want that we as well as they could come on a visit then go in a bath and there enjoy our love. That I could caress your penis. That you could touch my breast. That you could enter into me. That we would groan but not from a pain. That we would groan from love.

So it is a lot of desires. So it is a lot of feelings in my heart but I of nothing can make. I go to sleep and I sleep. My heart and a body burns and waits when I can be with you.

I LOVE YOU!!!

I WANT YOU!!!!

Yours and only your loving Ivana

Letter 39

[No Subject]   November 2

Hello My Lovely Man And My Sun!!!!!!

I have very much become missed without you. I am glad that you with me.

Yes we not together but we can communicate to speak about the dreams and it good from this idea when I present myself in your embraces that I am happy. It would be desirable to feel as you embrace me as we kissed.

Even when I watch TV think of us. You the best person in this world. You and only you the man of my dreams only with you I want to be together.

Only you and only with you!

I so happy that have found you. I never thought that a meeting of you so far but the god has given me chance and I have met you. I madly glad to this. Yes he has not given us opportunities to meet quickly but I feel soon we shall be together. I no know as but I think that very soon.

My darling tomorrow I shall go to the western union and I shall try to receive your help. I shall order tickets for November 8th, it is convenient for you?

My darling I shall ask in travel agency the name of flight and an arrival time to you.

Today was usual and only which I have received your letter has decorated of him.

I hope that soon I can feel your lips your gentle hands your love and tenderness and we shall enjoy love and happiness. These words it is impossible to transfer much but I know you understand me because our hearts feel one another.

I want you my lovely!

Yours and only yours forever Ivana

Letter 40

[No Subject]   November 3

Hello My Lovely Man And My Sun!!!!!!

I have very much become without you.

I never felt your hands never felt your kiss never was engaged in love and I want to make love only to you WOULD WANT THAT WE WILL BE TOGETHER!!!!!!!

My darling at me today was a lot of work and I did not have time to receive your help. Tomorrow I shall try to reach the western union.

I very much miss you and cannot fall asleep at night at once I think of you think of that as it would be fine if you were with me.

I want to feel you. As you caress me. As you touch to me. As you caress my breast. As you enter into me and we groan of pleasure and love.

My heart pricks when I think that you far and without me. I would want that we could enjoy life together. Well that I can receive your letters which calm me give me force and hope for our meeting.

I today on work am very tired but when received your letter all weariness has left.

I now want to go with you on the street to hold you for a hand to hear your gentle whisper your voice feel your breath and love.

My heart fire when I think of you about that as we shall make love.

Let us be everyone together as we shall have a rest from all that is filled usual day when we not together.

I love you and only you!

Yours forever, yours on all life Ivana

Letter 41

[No Subject]   November 4

Hello My Lovely Man And My Sun!!!!!

I very glad to receive your letter. Gentle and tender. I have very much become missed without you. That your arms are waiting all I need to hear.

Yesterday I say with mum in the evening. We much say about us with you. She speaks that is happy that now in my life there you. She say that wants to see us happy would want that our life was full of happiness and love. She is happy for us. She speaks when she looks at me even envies me that I have to which person I love with which I shall be happy. That now me have loving man who will care of me and with which I shall go on this life.

My darling today I have received your help for our tickets. Tomorrow I shall go to travel agency and shall order my tickets. I shall inform you the information of tickets tomorrow.

My darling now we with my mum eat to the grandmother. I shall say goodbye to my grandmother. My grandmother will be very glad to hear that I fly to you. I arrive tomorrow during the lunchtime from my grandmother. Already today have left from work.

All my friends on work are very happy for me. They wish our good luck. My darling I today went to my girlfriend and have told to her that on November 8th I already shall be at my favourite. Anna it has been very surprised and she too is very happy for us with you. Anna has told that will wait for a photo where we with you together.

I very much love you. You give me happy when I receive your letters the love the tenderness and sincerity.

I want to be with you and only with you. Today rain in the street but am happy. It is happy because I have you and love you!

I LOVE YOU!!!!

Yours and only your loving Ivana

Letter 42

[No Subject]   November 5

Hello my most gentle one!

How you today? I very glad to see your letter. I love you and very much miss on you. My darling I very much love you. I glad that already soon I shall be in your embraces. I happy up to tears that I can soon see and embrace you.

I very much wish to touch with the lips yours. I wish to give you the most sweet kisses.

My darling yesterday I was at my grandmother she has transmitted you a gift. It will be for you a surprise.

My grandmother bless us and wishes our good luck from bottom of the heart. My darling I think you like a gift to my grandmother. My darling I have arrived from my grandmother today and at once went in travel agency. Here the information on mine of the ticket which to me have informed in travel agency today.

Trip segment: Moscow (MOW) Atlanta (ATL)
Hartsfield Intl Arpt
Airline: Delta Air Lines   Flight: DL47
Depart: 08 November 2008, 13:10, Sheremetyevo Arpt
Arrive: 08 November 2008, 17:05, Hartsfield Intl Arpt

Trip segment: Atlanta (ATL) Moscow (MOW) Sheremetyevo Arpt
Airline: Delta Air Lines Flight: DL46
Depart: 07 May 2009, 15:30, Hartsfield Intl Arpt
Arrive: 08 May 2009, 10:30, Sheremetyevo Arpt

Much can be spoken about how people love each other. I all the night long thought what such the true love? I long could not fall asleep...because thought of it?

There are many stories and histories about the true strong love between the man and the woman. I think that the true love is not absolutely such situation when to the person it is good with other person. This moment is certainly important for love but I consider that there is an additional moment in which the sense of love consists. I think that love and still such condition when to the person it is bad without other person.

You agree with me? Because can be so that to you is good with any person and you think that it love but when this person leaves you becomes indifferent on it but if to you very badly and sadly without this person then this condition of soul also can be named LOVE. What you think of it?

To me it very sad without you. I can confidently tell that it is love. I LOVE YOU! I know that you too miss me. Thus we have mutual love the true love which will allow us to be happy. You agree with me? In this life the most important to understand that it is the true love and when the person understands it he becomes happy. I can be mistaken, but I so think. That you think of it? Tell to me please. I wish to know that you think.

I with impatience shall wait for your answer.

I love you and very much miss on you.

I very much hurry up to arrive to your gentle embraces.

Your gentle and loving Ivana

Letter 43

[No Subject]   November 6

Hello My Love and My Sun!

I very glad to receive your letter again. You do me happy constantly with each new letter. I so love you my Sun!!!! kiss kiss kiss!!

How you today? I hope what you are glad as well as I when you receive my letters? I cannot find words to explain my feelings and emotions when I see your letters. I so love you!! Thanks you that you do me such happy. Your love and your letters most pleasant in my days. Without you to me would not be so joyfully on a soul if you did not write to me. You understand my feelings? When I cannot see your letter I very much miss. Because I so love you!! kiss kiss kiss kiss!!

I again could not fall asleep at night yet have not presented you near to me. I have closed eyes have prepared for a kiss. I waited a touch of your lips to me. I hoped that there will be a miracle and I can receive your kiss. I so want it.

I already know that our first kiss will be very strong and long. You should prepare for it. I no joke!!! kiss kiss kiss I cannot kiss you yet consequently send to you many my kisses in the letter. I hope that you will receive it and will have pleasure. kiss kiss kiss kiss kiss kiss kiss kiss kiss kiss kiss kiss kiss kiss!

We will soon have the true kisses!!!!!!!

I so love you!!! Anna speaks to you "Hello". We have taken a walk yesterday not for long.

My darling now I send to Moscow. My darling I shall write to you tomorrow when arrive to Moscow.

I very much love you!

Your gentle and loving Ivana

Letter 44

[No Subject] November 7

My love. To me it is very bad now. I no know how to you this all to tell. I shall well speak you from the very beginning.

Today I have woken up in good mood. I have gone to embassy received the visa. Has passed interview. I was very happy. I thought that I shall be in your embraces already tomorrow.

I have gone to airport and there I was waited with bad news. Me, it is very bad. I choke with mental anguish. I do not represent that would be if I have come to the airport tomorrow. When I would go what to take my tickets. The girl which works there would tell to me for that tomorrow I could take off to you it is necessary for me in the consent with my visa I should have enough of money what to live in USA.

I have been very surprised not who earlier about it did not speak me. I could not think at all that there can be such rule. I the truth did not know about it!! To me have told that have entered this rule because some people leave there start so to steal the vagabond to be engaged in prostitution because at them not money for a life.

I explained to them that I shall live at you that we love each other and what money will be necessary for me but to me have told that a rule exist for all and it do what exceptions. I begged them. I explained to them we with you should be together but they do not listen to me speak me only one that that rules exist for all.

I no know that to us to do. I very much wish to be with you. I want to you. I wish you to see embrace to kiss. To tell to you strongly I love you.

To me so badly!!! I am upset. I do not understand our country such rules what for are necessary.

I very much love you. You are necessary to me only. I cannot live without you. I all life waited for you and here before us there was this barrier.

To me so it is bad. My eyes fill in bitter tears. Most me that I so have strongly brought you! But I knew that about it. My heart is broken off on a part from a pain. I cannot live without your love. I want to you my Sun. You have covered my life. You have made me happy. Only with you I have learned that such the true love!!!!!

You that for whom I waited all life. I adore you my charm. I do not have not enough you now as air. About as I want that you simply would embrace me. To me very hard and terribly here in the big city.

I feel helpless. I did not think I should be informed you such bad news. I thought that all behind and before us there are no not what barrier more.

That seems to me that I deliver you many problems it is very heavy to me to realize it. I feel myself very guilty to you. To me it is very bad. I cry at this time and me so painfully that it not tears of happiness and pleasure but tears of bitterness and the big mistake. I no know that to us to do!!!!

The size of the sum which should be together with my visa of 3000 dollars and still necessary 70 dollars for registration of papers. 3070 dollars are necessary that I could be with you. My love I no know where to me to take such money. All that at me remains it 184 dollars.

I do not understand our country. What for such rules!!!!!

I explained to them that with me not that does not happen but they speak that rules would exist that them to carry out instead of to stand and to not persuade them! They have told that from it not that will not leave and that what to stand to persuade them what to avoid these rules simply waste of time.

I thought all is passed wonderfully but now have big problem. I no know as me it to solve. I very much wish to be only with you. I all would give what to be with you. Not that it is not a pity to me for the sake of our happiness. Only together we shall be happy. I am tired to suffer. I wish to be happy to do you happy. I am tired to live suffering.

I love you my Sun!!!!

I understand to you big difficulty to help me there more for such short time but as soon as arrive to you I at once shall give you this money. I need to be shown only their presence to prove to them I can live in USA. Otherwise I cannot be tomorrow onboard the plane and I cannot take off to you my Sun.

I any more no know whether we can be in time up to tomorrow but I cannot go today at all to hotel and remain to spend the night at the airport what to save money.

I am in full confusion!!!

If you can assist us. I very much wish to be only with you forever. I wish to be always with you beside but I no know that to us to do.

I went today to bank and with have asked them in bank where branch western union? They to me have told at them is western union and they have explained to me where it to be. To me have told a remittance more than 1700 dollars I cannot receive. They have told that it will be necessary for me to receive a greater sum it will be necessary to divide on two parts.

I no know that to us to do. If you can send money through western union I can receive it tomorrow and take off to you my gentle prince. I any more no know as us it is possible to leave this position.

I shall not spend this money. I will need to be shown only them and when arrive to you at once shall give you them. I do not understand as us further to be. I very much wish to be with you.

My life without you is not necessary to me! I want to you my love. Is very a pity to me that so it has turned out. It is very a shame to me before you!

I hope you will have time to receive my letter. I very much worry. I hope you can help us my love. At me shivers all body shivering hands my heart pours blood. To me it is very sick that I deliver to you so much problems.

I love you wish to speak you it eternally!!! Forgive me my love!!!! I very strongly wish to be with you!!!!

I wait for your letter in Internet of café.

I LOVE YOU!!!!

Letter 45

[No Subject]   November 7

My darling I here wait for your letter. I no know that to me to do. I am guilty to you my love.

Forgive me...

Letter 46

[No Subject]   November 7

My darling you want what I would change tickets for other date? My darling please forgive to me that I no know only. I very much hurried up to arrive to you. I love you.

My darling all very dark now. I need to send to my city? My darling I do not wish to live without you. I VERY MUCH WISH TO BE WITH YOU.

I write to you now with tears on eyes. I cannot understand what for have thought up such severe rules. My darling if you could help me I would not spend this money. I need to be shown only it at customs. When I shall arrive I at once shall give them to you my darling.

To me it very bad from our powerlessness before such situation. I no know how to me to live without you. I had so much plans for our meeting and here all it has broken together with mine heart. Why we cannot be together my heart cannot understand it. It is very difficult to understand the law heart.

My darling I now on the Internet shall look forward to hearing from you.

Letter 47

[No Subject]   November 7

My darling I should feel not guilty. My darling I feel now that all my dreams break. I thought that tomorrow I can be already close with you. I very much require your love.

I have number you sent. I shall search for public telephone booth. I very much wish to hear your voice. I think that your voice will bring to my heart a lot of pleasure.

I now would not like to live at all. This life without you my love not necessary to me. I love you. To me it is very bad because I not can make for our meeting.

My darling I need to be shown only this money that they at me are. This money does not need to be spent it only for display. I no know who could give me such sum. I shall return right after stay to you. This money on what will be spent.

My darling why this world correct money? It not correct. What money us with you can share that. I do not wish to go down stream this severe world.

I wish to be near to you to enjoy in your gentle embraces.

I shall search for a public telephone booth at once.

Letter 48

[No Subject] November 7

My darling I ran on all to Moscow and searched for a public telephone booth but not that not could find as it very big city and could not leave far what to not lose the way. Here very malicious people. I shall continue the searches of public telephone booth tomorrow.

To me so it is terrible here one without you. I cannot so. I would give all that tomorrow already I could to nestle on you!!!! But I cannot make it. Why? Why between We have risen this barrier?

I love you wish to be only with you but for that we would be together we need to overcome last barrier. I no know how to us it to do. What to us to do my love? My darling I so wished to talk to you but at me at all it has turned out also.

I would not like to live in this severe world without you. I love you.

Only our love gives me force for a life further.

Mine the darling when already became late I have run in the airport have transferred mine start on Sunday.

Till Sunday we can something to think up? My darling it is necessary for me to show only this money for that me would miss to you.

I very much wish to be with you that it is not necessary any more.

My darling tomorrow morning as shall open the eyes I shall begin search of public telephone booth.

My darling I cannot live without you. This world not that attractive without you. You for me all in this life. You my happiness without you I not when I shall not be happy in this world.

I love you.

It is very a pity to me that people at customs do not understand me. I explained to them that you me love that when I arrive to you with me all will be good. I spoke them that they would write on yours e-mail and all have specified but they at all do not wish me to listen. They have asked me what I any more took away from them workers time have told that the law is the law. They speak what not as it is impossible to bypass it not what or another by.

These people not have hearts. I doubt such people can have someone to love. They do not find the true happiness because they do not have hearts cannot understand the person and to its shower as to it is bad.

Letter 49

[No Subject]   November 8

My darling I today as have woken up at once have gone on searches public telephone booth. I have found only one public telephone booth but he did not work. I shall continue searches of phone.

My darling is very a pity to me that we not that cannot make up to Sunday. I no know what now to do.

To me to go home?

I do not want home I wish be with you. I love you. To me very painfully to understand that we cannot be together.

I do not need to spend money more I need to be shown them only. If someone could lend them I could return them at once after arrival to you.

Why these people cannot understand that to me not my life without you is necessary? Why they speak that it is the law have thought up for what to protect citizens. They have thought up it the law for that what to exhaust people!!! I do not understand many rules in this mad city. My darling now I am very tired I shall go to sleep on to road I shall look a public telephone booth. My prince I shall write tomorrow when I shall wake up.

Letter 50

[No Subject]   November 9

Hello my darling

Tomorrow I shall go to Tair home. I not so wish to leave. I wish to be with you beside more likely but I understand our powerlessness above this situation.

My darling now I shall run in.

The airport what to have time to change tickets. I shall transfer date start for November, 22nd. You wanted what I would transfer for November, 22nd?

My darling I at all do not represent as my mum will be surprised to see me. She likely thinks that we already together. I very much hope that we can be together fast.

I shall write to you after I change tickets. I shall go now to the airport.

Letter 51

[No Subject] November 9

My darling I now have come at once from the airport to the Internet of café.

What to write to you. I am forced to ask from you the help for trip home. My darling if I not was in the city I would not ask from you not that.

My darling understand my situation. I changed already two times my tickets and overpaid for them each time 15 percent. Now I have transferred tickets till November 22nd.

My darling to me it is very terrible to remain here in Moscow. It is huge city. I have not got used to such way of life. Here all people malicious also are occupied.

The business. At me remains money only on that what to write to you still some times. I no know that to me to do. I cannot here to find work for that what not many to earn on a way back and to pay habitation.

My darling I now have given last money of what to me have changed tickets. My darling it is necessary for me to pay for a room where to stay of 250 dollars and on road up to house about 200 dollars.

Here in to Moscow very huge prices. This city very much is not pleasant to me. It very much wild and severe. Residing here costs much. My darling I shall spend money which have remained with me even on that what to attempt. I shall leave that money which at me are on the Internet of café.

It is very terrible to me to remain one in another's city.

I very much want to be warmed in your gentle embraces.

Now in the street is colder. My darling I very much wish to fall into your embraces. My darling it on my fault such situation has turned out. My darling thanks you that you at me is.

Now I shall go what not many to have a sleep and write to you tomorrow.

Letter 52

[No Subject] November 10

Mine lovely when I went to the western union to me have told that the address for that what to send the help is not necessary to you my name only.

I rented the apartment in Moscow what to spend the night there at me is no money to pay for her. The owner has taken away from me the passport and has told that will give when I shall return money for apartment. My darling I need to pay 250 dollars for an apartment and on road up to the house about 200 dollars. I have very few money am afraid that at me money even will soon not pay for the Internet of café.

My darling I today attempted only two pies with a potato and coffee. I afraid to spend all of money then I cannot even write to you. My darling to me it is very terrible.

I want home. I want warm food. My darling think up that not be.

I look forward to hearing from you here.

Letter 53

[No Subject]   November 10

My darling you need to send your help on my country Rosiija. I can receive it at any office of the western union. To me have told it there. Try do AS I speak you. I have not enough time. My darling understand that at me how many money at all will not be fast. To me it very terrible. My darling only our love helps me to live further. I love you. My darling I need to be sent the help in the same way as last time.

Letter 54

[No Subject]   November 10

My darling to me have told that you can send the help as last time. To me have told in the western union that I will not have problems about their reception. If you very much wish to know the address I shall go learn but it to be not close and at me will leave for this time. We have not enough time. I need to pay for an apartment more if I shall be late in Moscow.

Letter 55

[No Subject]   November 10

My darling I very much love you. Thanks you for everything that you do for our love. You the person about which I dreamed.

My darling I shall do all as you speak. I love you. I hope that we can be together this month. I very much wish to concern you. I wish to present you the kisses.

My darling soon shall begin for room at once I shall go home. I now very much want home. I feel here as the tramp.

My love I very much miss on you. My darling tomorrow I shall come in the Internet of café.

Letter 56

[No Subject]   November 11

Hello my darling. I have received your help. My darling I very glad that now I can to go home.

I shall write to you when I shall be in the town. I love you. I hope that on November, 22nd I shall be in your embraces.

My darling thanks for everything that you do for our happiness.

I thank the god that we have found each other.

My darling soon at me already a train need to go. I shall write to you more when home.

Well? I love you.

Thanks my love.

Letter 57

[No Subject] November 12

Hello My Love and My Sun!

I very glad to receive your letter today. Thanks you that you do not forget about me and continue to write to me. I very much love you and want in your embraces!

My darling I have arrived to mine town 3 hours back. I have come all over again home. My mum has been very surprised to see me she thought that we already together with you. My darling when I have seen mum mum have asked why we not together. I have explained to her about that has happened. My mum too very much was upset but I has told that we shall be with you together on November, 22nd.

How you today? What did you have today for fun? I thought of you and missed. My mum speak to you "Hello" and that you watched weather because an autumn and possible to catch a cold.

I have told to mum that I care of you and will not allow you to be ill!! I hope what you are not going to be ill now? Because I will long. I no want that you were ill - you understand me?

I wait for you every night in my bed that you have warmed me have gently embraced. I very much want it. And you? You think of me also? You want that we heated each other in cold nights?

I do not wish to be more lonely. I do not wish to fall asleep and wake up without you! I very much love you and I want to you! I no know as me to express love because words simply do not suffice for this purpose. I hope what you do not take offence at me for it?

I think that we will be together soon and I do not wish to think that between us the big distance. It will not prevent our big love. You agree with me?

My heart wishes to fight near to your heart. I want this moment with impatience. You and only you are necessary for my heart. I cannot name now my heart lonely because I have you!

We are not lonely any more!!! Because we love each other!!!! kiss kiss.

I will wait for your answer tomorrow.

I love you!

Your gentle and loving Ivana

Letter 58

[No Subject]   November 13

Hello my darling.

To me very sadly to hear from you that we cannot be together on November 22nd. I very much wish to be with you. My darling unfortunately I have no that person who could assist me with that huge sum. I has given everything that at me is for our happiness.

My darling when I represent on the barrier we wash the face there are tears. I no know as me to overcome this huge ocean.

It is very a pity to me that I cannot elementary hear your voice at all. If I could even hear to you the darling for me a voice. My darling I cannot understand laws of my state. They are very severe.

I no know as us all it to overcome.

I love you. I would give the life for our happiness. My darling without you in my life is not present happiness. I consider that happiness when you are beside with favourite person can speak him all fine words looking him in the face.

My darling I wish to admire your fine eyes and to sink in them. I require your love. Without you I do not represent the life. My life is necessary to whom she is not necessary to me without you. You sense of my life.

Without you I shall live on the ground without pleasure.

I shall be only happy near to you. I shall search for a way to call to you. I no know where to me it to find in mine town there is no public telephone booth. I shall try something to think up. I very much wish to hear your voice my prince.

You for me everything without you is necessary for me of that.

I am ready to live with you in poverty ready to be with you in any vital situation. I know that being with you all shall be equally happy.

My darling I love you and shall love only you eternally.

Your love Ivana

Letter 59

[No Subject]   November 14

Hello My Love and My Sun!

Today I have joyful mood again because I can see your letter. Thanks you that you do me happy! kiss kiss.

My darling to me very sadly that we not together in November. I very much wish to be with you. For me this main thing. I thought that it necessary to come back home a bad sign.

I pray to the god that he would help us to meet.

My visa really b2. My darling I no know that to us now to do. My darling when in Moscow to me have explained that is not present not what other way to pass customs. There is a unique way that I would have 3000 dollars on residing at your country. They have explained to me that they are not assured that to me is where there to live.

I have told that at my favourite and asked them to write to you but to me have told that there is no not what other way except for presence at itself the necessary sum.

They at all did not wish to listen to me have asked that I would not take away from them their workers time. My darling I no know that to me now to do. I very much wish to behave in your hands but would like to cry. I try to be strong. I hope we shall overcome all obstacles which against our love.

Today there was very interesting day for me. At first I have woken up also to me it seemed that you near to me in a bed because about me someone laid but then I have looked and have seen that it lays a pillow which I embraced at night when thought of you. I represented you near to me. I think of you constantly want that the pillow has turned to you that I could tell to you many words which I wish to tell.

I very much love you very much would like to be now near to you embrace kiss never to let off!!!!

I have gone about a bus stop there was a pair which long kissed at all on eyes and it was unimportant that other people look at a bottom.

I want that we kissed also you. And you? I think that all will look also at us and to envy us.

And after work also went joyful to the Internet of café to share with you my good impressions for a today.

I very much love you and I do not want that you forgot it.

Tomorrow I will go to the grandmother. I will tell to her "Hello" from you necessarily. I will answer you on Sunday.

Your gentle and loving Ivana

Letter 60

[No Subject] November 16

When I have received your letter my heart has not stopped nearly. It till now pricks. Only the love which lives in my heart can cure all pain because she pure and light. From your letter I was in a shock. To me became now even worse. I did not expect to hear from you it! I even could not think that you do not trust me. I always with you was fair. I count that the most terrible is lie. For me the most terrible sin it to deceive whom that I love. I hate lie it so is dirty.

And now you speak me it! You have hurted me very much. What for you so with me? Mine eyes in tears.

I no know that to me to do. I do not know as me to live after that. Me not who did not do so painfully.

But I forgive you because I very much love you. I know that I shall be with whom except for you is happy. Tell to me that it is necessary to make and I shall make all. I at all do not understand such customs scam. What did you wish to tell it? Tell to me it.

Know that without you my life is not meaningful. I no know that with me will be if I shall not be with you. I wish to see always you with me beside.

I look at your photos and I speak myself what you fine. I conceal when I look in your fine eyes. I would want that you always were happy and that on your charming face always there would be your gentle smile!

Yours and only yours Ivana

Letter 61

[No Subject]   November 17

To me till now it is bad. I yesterday could not fall asleep. I all the night long cried. I no know that to me to do and as to me to live further. I did not understand why you so with me address I in fact love you would do all that we were together.

That is a pity to me that so it has turned out. I understand you that you so spoke me. I very strongly love you and on it my heart is ready to forgive you my prince but what for you spoke me such words? Whether I no know I can sometime forget it. To me so it is bad since that moment as I have received your letter from mine eyes tears did not vanish. So still nobody humiliated me. I understood that I did not wish to trust that it was written by you. I not when did not think that you can tell to me such. I not when not whom did not deceive. For me it is the big shame. I read yours to letters and thought that it is written not by you. All your other letters as if written by absolutely different two persons. In them of that is peculiar to you. No matter what state department say I was forced to show money for trip. This the truth. Customs was very severe with me as spoke you.

In you only feelings of love tenderness you the most tender charming the man in the world. I love you all heart!!! I very much wish to be with you and shall make all for the sake of it.

I always trusted you I is mad in you would make all for the sake of you and now I wish to trust you all my heart. I would like to shout from a pain she breaks off my heart on pieces. To me so it is bad. I all have got confused.

All that I know now that I madly love you!!!! I wish to be with you.

I would no know that with me yesterday if I did not trust in that all will be good. I shouted I cried my heart was ready to jump outside to me so it is bad not when was not.

I should speak with whom my mum asked that happens but I could tell to her of that because I did not have words I as if have lost for nothing of speech. I choked with a pain. To me was so badly!!!!

About as though I wished to be now in your gentle embraces simply to forget about all this.

I want to you!!! I cannot live without you!!!!

I love you. I wish to speak you it eternally!!! I would want that we always were together. All our life. I would want that we carried together all pleasures troubles in our life. I love you and shall make all for the sake of that what to be with you.

I would want that you were the happiest the man in the world. I shall make all for the sake of it!!!!

I forgive you my love. I shall transfer this insult! I shall carry all for the sake of you but I ask you do not act so more with me!

I with impatience shall wait for your following letter!!!

I love you!!

I grieve on you!!!

I gently embrace you and is sweet the whole!!!

Letter 62

[No Subject]   November 18

Hello My Love and My Sun!

I so glad that you have written to me and now a smile on my face because you have sent me the finest birthday wishes.

I so love you!!!!! Thanks that you give me happiness and smiles!!!!

My darling what to me to do with our tickets? They are ordered for November 22nd? I have learned in travel agency that they can change date of a start.

I so missed on you. Every night it is difficult to me to fall asleep because I cannot sleep without you. I think of you constantly. And how you fall asleep? You think of me too? I very much want that we could fall asleep easy together to see each other before a dream and after a dream. I so want it.

All my girlfriends and mum say that I have found my happiness which I so long searched. I searched to you because you my happiness my big love.

Thanks you that you give me your love and tenderness!!!! I

will try to make very much you the happiest man in the world!!!!!!

I hope that I can make it and we can carry out all our dreams in a reality. All will look at us rejoice to our happiness and even now when I write you this letter I am happy because you have made me happy!!! kiss kiss kiss kiss.

You prepare your lips for our first and longest sweet kiss???

mmmmm kiss kiss kisss kissss kissss.

Today in the street very beautiful weather. There is no cold but also there is no dampness. In the street it is a lot of snow and all trees are covered by beauty. It pleases me very much.

I hope that you have many smiles today and will think of me.

I so love you!!!!

Your gentle and loving Tatyana

Letter 63

[No Subject] November 19

Hello My Lovely Man and My Sun!!!!!!!

My darling I have here as though second name Tatyana. So my grandmother likes to name me. This tender name.

I think only of you about that as it will be good us together. I very much would want that our life will be fine. What you would want that I made when we shall be together? I think of you much. I want say to you about that as I present our usual day when we shall be together.

I think that it will begin as we shall wake up with you in one bed. I shall lay the head on your breast and you will embrace me the hand. I shall open eyes shall see you. I shall tender kiss you and you too will wake up will answer my kisses gentle and passionate. Then I shall stand from a bed. I shall be naked dress your shirt go to prepare on kitchen easy breakfast for us. When I shall prepare for it you come for me behind and your embraces will warm me you will kiss me all over again in an ear then in a neck your hands will caress my body my breasts my hips but here the teapot will begin to boil and we shall have breakfast with you.

Then we shall take a shower together. We shall make love in a bath and only then we shall leave. We will have good mood all day will be fine.

Then when you will come from work I shall meet you the gentle kiss. We with you shall make all together. In the evenings we shall sit on sofa near TV to look good film then together go to a bedroom make love yet weariness.

I VERY MUCH WOULD WANT THAT IT HAPPENED FASTER!!!!!!!

If at whom that from us will be bad mood that we shall try to change it. If you will long that I shall make all that you smiled and melancholy have disappeared from your eyes. I shall make all that you always were happy and I hope that you too.

I love you my life belongs to you.

How you imagine our usual day together? Or weekend? Or a holiday?

I with impatience wait for your letter.

Yours and only your loving Ivana

Letter 64

[No Subject]   November 20

Hello My Lovely Man and My Sun!!!!

I very much miss you all day very glad when I receive your letter. I with impatience wait for our meeting and I hope that it soon happen. I very much want to be with you.

Today I prepared for supper of a house and thought as it would be good if you too could try that I have made. I cooking soup from meat beets carrots onion other spices. It name to Borsch. You heard about it? I think that this most well known dish in Russia after pel'menis and pancakes.

I was going on the second mashed potatoes with a cutlet and roast. I have cooked compote from dried apples with sugar was very tasty. I so would like that you have tried my dishes could estimate their taste would think that was pleasant to you. I like to prepare adore to prepare for delicacies. For example a pizza pies a shish kebab many other things. I name their delicacies because not so frequently for them I prepare.

My darling if I shall transfer my tickets for February, 7th what to do with visa? The visa has been given to me for 6 months. My darling I no know that to me to do. At us is what not be a way to be together earlier?

I very much want to stand on kitchen and feel as you embrace me kiss touch my hips help me to be going. You would help me? I hope what yes.

I with impatience wait for your letter. I hope that today's dream will be fine also you as well as I will see in the dream a fine meeting of us with you.

I love you.

Yours and only yours Ivana

Letter 65

[No Subject]   November 21

Hello My Lovely Man and My Sun!!!!!!

I glad to receive your letter. I with impatience waited for it both my heart was warmed also my heart knocked when I today have opened it.

My darling I am good now I go in travel agency shall change my date of a start for February 1st. My darling I very much hope that we can be together.

Tomorrow I cannot write to you. Tomorrow I shall go to village to my grandmother. I learn I cannot renew my work in hospital my place there taken.

I think of that as it would be good if could in weekend go on a nature have a rest there. I will cook tasty salads. We would take with ourselves tent knifes and all other accessories to a campaign and have put in the machine. I have taken a bottle red wine. I do not love alcohol but a red wine I drink on holidays but not much. We would take meat what to fry it on a fire would go to a wood or on seacoast.

Where you would want? I would like closer to water. There we would put tent grow a blanket what to sit on it. Would put on a table salads a wine glasses have dissolved a good fire. Then together would swim in water to lake or the river. The main thing that we could swim together. We would bathe laid on a coast kiss. Caress one another. Enjoy a nature. Looked at the sky. Have then returned to tent have prepared for meat and would sit to have supper.

A fire shine us. You open a bottle pour a wine in glasses. We drink a little for us I see that one droplet has remained on your lips kiss you gently. You respond on my kiss take me on hands carry in tent. We are engaged in love we enjoy each second of love each minute of passion and it is very good us together.

Then we leave tent categorize a blanket closer as a coast and we look at the sky. You embrace me warm the heat. We are closer and closer we speak fall asleep under singing night birds under a night rustle of leaves.

I think that soon all of what we dream the reality begins. Each our day will be filled with love and we shall be happy forever. I love you send you the most sweet kisses and hope that they warm you at cold night in your bed.

If when you read my letter and in the night look at sky there you will see constellation the big she-bear as a ladle. I send you this ladle full kiss and tenderness.

I love you!

Yours and only yours Ivana

Letter 66

[No Subject]   November 23

Hello My Love and My Sun!!!!

I very much missed on you. How you? I love you hope that you will receive my kisses together with this letter…kiss kiss kiss kiss.

I have well visited the grandmother. Excuse that I have not written to you yesterday. When we have arrived to the grandmother weather was cold and the grandmother at once has offered us hot tea with honey. I have very much frozen consequently not has refused hot tea.

What did you have interesting? I thought about to you all the day long all the night long. It is a pity that you were not a line with me. I so wanted it.

I very much love you and wish to appear in your gentle embraces. And you? I hope what you do not happen sad? I do not want that you had bad mood. I want that you every day had many smiles of happiness when you think of me.

The grandmother asked about you much. She speaks to you "Hello" and my mum too. They are glad for us wish our good luck and big infinite love.

When I went to bed I have taken from the grandmother the second pillow that I could embrace it. You have guessed what for I wished to embrace a pillow? I thought of you and has presented that I embrace you!!!!! And consequently I slept it is very sweet because you were a line with me and I could embrace you!! It is my dream but I have tried to carry out it in a reality. You do something similar?

All my love my dreams only for you!!! Because I love you also I wish to make you the happiest person!! Because you already has made me happy that has presented me your love and tenderness!!! Thanks!!!! I kiss you gently on the mouth...kiss kiss kisss.

I with impatience wait for your answer tomorrow.

Your gentle and loving Ivana

Letter 67

[No Subject] November 24

Hello My Love and My Sun!!!

How you today? What did you have interesting this day? I very much miss on you and now I so is glad that you have written to me. I love you!!!

Today I again could not fall asleep at night but as in the street beautiful weather. I have gone to a court yard to take a breath of fresh air to look at stars. It so is beautiful. I no know that with me happen but I could not sleep. Do not worry please. I did not depart far from my house. I was about the house. It appears night air so is fine. I enjoyed it but it is a pity that without you.

You would like to leave with me on street at night? I do not like to go at night in the street but with you I would go anywhere because I love you and to me it is terrible nothing with you.

I would take your hand then the second hands would ask a sweet gentle kiss. It would be the most romantic kiss. You only present in night. In the street bright stars and the moon and we with you stand under this beautiful light enjoy the friend the friend. I would like it now!!!!! And you? What do you think of it?

Then we would come to the house I would prepare for us tea. Before a dream it is necessary to go to a shower. You understand about what I speak? We would go to a shower would deliver each other the most gentle sweet pleasures. mmmmmm kiss kiss.

I so want it! I love you and very glad that we will be together!!! You have presented to me a lot of happiness and smiles!! I never was such happy!!!! Thanks you for it!!!

I LOVE YOU and I THINK Of YOU every DAY, EACH HOUR, every MINUTE and SECOND. For me the BIGGEST HAPPINESS IS to be with YOU and to ENJOY YOU!!!!

You understand my feelings? I hope that to a smog to see your letter tomorrow. I will look forward it.

Your gentle and loving Ivana

Letter 68

[No Subject] November 25

Hello My love!

I very much love your letter as it always filled with love and to worry about me. Very much it was pleasant to me has me heated up. I very much thaw when I read your letter knowing you are lonely now. I was very good to know that this such.

It is very sad that we not together my love. As it would be desirable so urgently to have strong embraces.

But I know that somewhere there behind of ocean there is a person liked to me. It would be desirable with which the cinema is possible to look and to speak about life and a lot of friend. And to have an entertainment and laughter. And to fall asleep in embraces in the evening. And to waken give a soft kiss in the morning to see smiling of loved person.

My love. I want to see you soon my love. Now I to go to sleep and think of you. The love for you prays also.

Kissssss and Hugsssssss!

Yours Galina

Letter 69

[No Subject]   November 26

Hello My Lovely Man and Sun!!!!!!!!

I glad to receive your warm letter very much miss on you would want that we with you were together. You in my heart. I love you!!!!

Today at night a remarkable dream has dreamed me. It was fine dream about us with you. To me has dreamed as though I and you walked on quay. We had a bottle of champagne and a few fruit. We for a long time walked at territory of the sea then have stopped in one very beautiful place where there was no person. We have settled down about the sea. We have opened a bottle of champagne. Small balls of gas of champagne played as if small luminous moths. They were poured on the Sun, everyone by the color. It was magnificent. And during that moment we were the happiest people in the world. To us was so well that us all world around did not interest. Our hearts fought on one frequency. We embraced kissed. We were close on so much on how many it only is possible.

I was happy that was very good us but when I have woken up have understood that it was only dream. I did not want to wake up because I know you are not present now with me beside but it will proceed not for a long time as we soon shall be together.

My darling Ivana in translation Galina Russian angel of love. It is very a pity to me that you have not understood me. I want to be only with you. I love you you the man of my dream and I want to be with you!!!!

Your loving and gentle Ivana

Letter 70

[No Subject]   November 27

Hello my darling!!

I very much miss!!! As has passed your day today? I hope that successfully. Why you today not written to me???

Today I saw you in the dream. We walked on very beautiful park. This park was not familiar to me in it there were no people except for us with you. We walked on park only together. When have woken up have woken up with a smile on the person.

My mum speaks that I today spoke in a dream and named your name. Today waited when I shall see your letter. I very much hurried up in the Internet of café but I was upset when did not see your letter. I hope that tomorrow you write to me.

I worry. I no know that to me to think.

Letter 71

[No Subject]   November 28

Hello my dear!

My darling I am very strong on you I miss. I dream of that much time when we can be together and enjoy each minute lead together.

Recently I see that you write to me less than earlier. You are occupied by work?

My darling there is no worse a torture to not see from you news. It is very bad to me to be in a distance from you. I to a pain wish to be near to you. I wish to kiss embrace you. I wish to enjoy long minutes in your gentle embraces. It is very a pity to me that now we are deprived all this. I cannot wait for that happy moment when I can run in your embraces.

At me very much big insult on this world that we not be together. Why this world not fair to loving people?

This life without you is not necessary to me and all this world is not necessary to me without your love. You my unique love. Without you for me is not present happiness.

My darling I shall go to the grandmother to village and

bring her with themselves in Tair. On Monday I my mum and the grandmother shall go to bank take to court for our meeting. My darling I hope that the god will help us. I very much hope that at us all to turn out and I shall have the necessary sum of what to fly to you.

I love you.

Your love for a century Ivana

Letter 72

[No Subject] November 30

Hi my love!!!

How are you? How weather at you?

My mum asked me that I transferred you big and ardent greetings.

Accept from me my sincere wishes of good mood most sincere hot kisses also my strong hot embraces.

I very much miss on you my love!!! I so want our meeting with you my Beloved Prince!!! I all life dreamed of such person as you. For me to think of you each minute is big pleasure!!! To think of the loved person is a great pleasure!!! My ideas about our meeting do not give me sleep!!! I so want to see you my love!!! I very much want that when I opened eyes in the morning you was always with me beside!!!

You would like it my charm?

I expect day when I shall see you my love!!! To me my love would be desirable to present you full pleasure our first night with you!!!

You would like it, my beloved?

My darling today I have arrived home together with my grandmother. Tomorrow we shall go three together to bank to ask to court for our meeting.

My love to you grows with each minute!!!

And now I finish my letter with ideas on you my love!!!

Yours Ivana!!!

Letter 73

[No Subject]   December 1

Hi my sweetheart!!!

How are you? At me all is good. How weather at you?

I very grateful to destiny that I have found you my love!!! Each day brings to me huge pleasure when I see your letter!!! Your letters for me something the greater than the letter!!! For me is a huge happiness to see your letter in mine e-mail! What for you my letters mean?

My favourite today we went to bank ask to court for that that I could to arrive to you. To us have told in bank that on the request courts will consider our application. To me have told that results to me will be known this week.

When I wake up I think of you my love!!! When I fall asleep I think of you!!! When we shall be together with you I shall be the happiest woman on the Earth!!!

I very much want to be with you my love!!! You want that I was with you? I very much miss on you!!! You miss on me my love?

I think that it is very good when you really like and appreciate persons! And for me the most important person is YOU!!! I LOVE YOU AND I SHALL LIKE!!!

I SHALL BE YOURS FOREVER, MY PRINCE!!!

YOU MY GENTLE AND TENDER PRINCE!!!

YOURS FOREVER IVANA!!!

Letter 74

[No Subject] December 2

Hi my sweetheart!!!!

I very glad to receive from you the letter today. I always glad to your letters mine prince. They always lift my mood.

For me was the big happiness to meet such person as you my sweet. You became my ideal my star of captivating happiness and I glad that you have taken a place in my big hot female heart.

Love I cannot be without you for me it more begins torture. I want to be near to you want to feel your gentle touches kisses want to hear from you gentle words of love.

Dear I want to prepare for our meeting. What you think of it my sweet prince? I think we have learned each other already enough and it is time to us to pass to the following stage of our relations. I think that we may learn about each other more if we shall lead any time together my lovely.

My love to you is very strong and serious I not so small girl to play games.

I very much want to meet you my prince and hope that our desires coincide.

My love you want to meet me at you houses????? On it I shall finish this letter. I wait for your fast reply my loved.

I send you a gentle kiss and strong embraces.

With all love your sweet Ivana!!!!!!

Letter 75

[No Subject] December 3

Hi my love!!!

How are you? At me all is good. How weather at you? I very much miss on you my love. You miss on me my charm? My darling tomorrow I shall go to bank and find out the information concerning mine courts for our meeting.

I very much hope that the bank to agree to help to meet us. I very much wish to be in your embraces as soon as possible.

I constantly dream of our meeting with you my love. I very much want that when I have arrived to you we have lead pleasant evening at any restaurant. Also danced slow dance under music Robert Miles. You would like it my love? I very much would want it.

I very much would like to present you a longest kiss that has felt all sweet of my fine lips. I very much want that you have felt my gentle and strong embraces.

I always dreamed of such person as you my love and very much would like that we were near to you my love. I feel the small girl who has fallen in love with you without memory.

To me it very sad without you without your embraces and gentle tender kisses.

I very much want to be with you my Prince!!!

I so want it!!!!

With huge love and with all my tenderness yours Ivana!!!

Letter 76

[No Subject]   December 4

My darling at me sad news. Today we went to bank in occasion of courts. To me have told that refuse in court. I no know that to me to do.

To me have told that they cannot give me such huge sum to court because I shall not have an opportunity to pay it from the wages.

Dear I very much wish to be with you for Christmas and New Year. I do not wish to be far from you for holidays. At us in Russia speak as you will meet New Year and it will lead.

My darling I very much wish to be in your embraces as soon as possible. I wish to be with you you for me all. You for me both air and water. I can live without water and food but cannot live without love.

I do everything what to be together but at me it is impossible to arrive to you. I asked my grandmother to sell its house. I no know how many its house will cost but I think that it is very cheap. The house of the grandmother very old and to be in small villages.

My darling I am ready on everything what to be with you. I

would try any ways for that we were together. You can something to think up?

My darling I very much wish to hear your voice very much miss on you. I love you. To me it is very bad without you.

I shall go tomorrow to the city of Cheboksary to search there for a public telephone booth. I wish to hear your voice. I think it will please me. I shall be happy though on half when I shall see your voice.

I require your love. I wish to embrace you to present you the most gentle kisses. I dream to meet these winter holidays together. To me very painfully to understand that we cannot be together because of what that of money.

It kills me.

Letter 77

[No Subject] December 5

My love!!!

I so is glad that you have written the letter!!!!!! I no know the public telephone booth will work but shall go to city of Cheboksary. Mine are favourite I shall be pleased much to hear your voice.

I very much love you and adore you!!!!! I want to be with you each day!!! To wait for you from work!!!! I want to prepare you for breakfast and supper each day!!!!! And to wake up in the mornings together with you!!!!! Each day to love you all life!!! I want to be mother of your children to love them just as you!!!!!!!!!! I want you - I want that our family was very happy!!!!!!!!!!! I know that we shall be with you forever!!!

I LOVE YOU MY LOVED!!!!!!!!!!!! I YOURS!!!!!!!!!!!!!

IN MY IDEAS AND SOUL ONLY YOU MY LOVE!!!!!!!!!!!!!!!!

I SHALL WAIT FOR YOUR LETTER With LOVE!!!!!!!!!

Yours forever Ivana

Letter 78

[No Subject]   December 6

Hello My Lovely Man and My Sun!!!!

My darling I very much miss on you. I very much wish to touch you in my dreams. You my most desired dream. It is very a pity to me that I can be with you now only in the dreams and the happiest dreams.

I love you. I wish to be close with you always. I hope that we can lead holidays together. My darling I do not wish to be far for Christmas from you.

My darling I very much wish to hear your voice. I hope that at us it will turn out to speak by phone even.

I love also the whole yours Ivana

Letter 79

[No Subject] December 7

Hi my darling!

I very strongly miss on you. To me very sadly to think of that we not together. My dear when I think of that I still was fast I can in your embraces on my eyes appear the darling know when all our dreams can be valid in our life.

It is very a pity to me that now I can dream only about a touch to you.

I no know that you play on the guitar. I very much would wish to listen as you play on the guitar.

My darling I cannot live without you. My life without love has what sense. I live hope that all will be fast well and we shall find a way to overcome all obstacles risen on our way.

Our love helps me to live in this severe world. I would give all for our love and for our happiness. My darling for you I am ready on all. To me it very sick that I cannot make for our meeting. I hope that all is fast to change.

We should be together it is our destiny.

I love you and I shall love eternally only you.

You my destiny.

I miiiiiiissssssssss.......

Yours and only your loving and gentle Ivana

Letter 80

[No Subject]   December 8

I hope that that all will be well and very soon we shall be together forever. I very strongly love you. I very much would want that we were together I cannot live without you. I very much would want that we were together forever. You for me the most important man in the world. I cannot live without you. I very much wish to be with you every day.

I dream of your sweet kisses gentle embraces. I very strongly love you. About as I wish to speak you it every day. I hope that very soon I can speak you it every day much many times.

Today my day has passed well. I all the day thought of you my gentle prince!!!!

The dream dreamed me last night and in this dream we beat together you and I!!!! It was a fine dream.

We with you together in the cozy house. Around of this house a wood. Not far from it there a river. There very beautiful nature. We with you were there together around of us whom was. We sat with you and drank tea. Then we have gone to walk. We walked on avenue keeping for hands. I went and joked, we laughed. On our faces there was a smile.

We went where that far to depth of a wood but suddenly we have stopped and began to look against each other. I looked in your eyes in them there were so much passions. You looked at me and I simply thawed in your sight. I could not come off from your pure as morning dew of eyes. Us pulled to the friend to the friend. We came nearer also our bodies were weaved in embraces. I felt your hot kisses. You so passionately kissed me. You kissed my neck ironed my body touched my hair. We were covered with passion. We could not come off from each other. We kissed very long.

Suddenly you have told to me that you know a fine place and we have gone there. You went put off me. Suddenly I have felt gentle embraces you have closed my eyes we moved some steps when you have opened my eyes I have seen before myself a remarkable glade. It so has liked me. It was not the greater glade on coast of lake.

We have approached to coast and have laid down on the ground. I have turned to you we began to kiss. I covered you with kisses. We were very long on this glade we kissed embraced.

We have not noticed as has passed time and in the street became already dark. Then we have laid down on a back holding each other for hands looked in the sky. On it there were many stars. Light of the moon fell on your face. I laid and admired you.

Suddenly you ask me to look at the sky. I have lifted a head upwards you to me have shown a finger on constellation!!!

This constellation was similar to a flower and you have told that this flower for me!!!!

On it I have woken up. When I have opened eyes was very a pity to me that it only a dream but this dream was fine is real so much. I hope that that very soon a love washing all our dreams will be executed also we shall be together forever!!!!

I very strongly love you!!!! I very much wish to be with you.

You my destiny. I want to you, I want to you. I wish you to see to embrace to kiss and give you all caress and tenderness every day. When we shall be together we shall be the happiest pair in the world!!!

I madly love you!!!! I with impatience shall wait for your letter!!!!

I gently embrace you and passionately whole.

I hope that I can soon do it every day!!!

Letter 81

[No Subject]   December 9

Hi my love!!!

How are you? How weather at you?

I am heated in heat of your letters and dreams about day that I can hold you in my hands and show you it.

I worry about you and I love you. I feel warm heat your soul I feel the strong need for you to have an effect and IS SHOWN that you like.

Your letters always bring to me huge pleasure, my love. I feel to you a huge attraction and huge love which reduces me from mind.

I so wait for our meeting with you!!! I dream of our meeting!!! I wait for our meeting with you!!! I want our meeting with you!!! And I want to tell you that I love you!!!

I finish my letter to you with ideas on you!!!

Yours Ivana!!!

Letter 82

[No Subject] December 9

Hi My love!

I very much to love your letter because it always filled with love and care for me. Very much it pleased me and warmed. I want the one long strong kiss as you say. I want to tell that I love you.

Because I always want my husband would love me. I like that in your letters the love to me is felt. I very much to thaw when to read about your loneliness because I was very good to know that this such.

It is very sad that we not together my love because it would be desirable so strongly to have strong embraces. It would be desirable to be near the loved and native person.

My love I want to fall asleep in your embraces in the evening wake up give it to you in the morning soft kiss see smiling person of the loved person my love. I want to see you soon my love and me it is sad that we with you now not together my love.

I finish my letter to you with all my tenderness and love.

Yours Ivana!!!

Letter 83

[No Subject]   December 11

HELLO MY LOVE!!!

My darling I yesterday went in the city of Cheboksary that would call to you. Dear I very much wished to hear your voice. I love you.

To me it is very bad because yesterday have spent in vain time for a trip to Cheboksary. I could not hear your voice. My darling why you speak what to us impossible to meet? I do not wish even to think of it.

It is necessary for us 3000 dollars only for one or two days of what to show them. This money does not need to be spent. I no know what to do. If who could lend that to us we would return it. When I to you shall arrive all sum will be reliably kept at me.

My darling I do not wish to realize that we cannot be together. This life without you is not necessary to me. Without you I not when cannot find out happiness.

My darling up to our happiness has remained only one step. I do not wish to trust that we cannot make this last step to our meeting.

For me it is not simple words. I not when did not love as I love you. Likely all these troubles strengthen my love. I all more wish to be with you more.

I recollect as I lived without you. My life was simply grey and not cheerful. I did not see a life. You have presented me a new life. You have opened to me a door in a fairy tale of love. You have presented me the most sweet dreams. I all shall give that all our dreams would become real. I am ready to give a life only for what to touch you to look in your fine eyes.

I do not wish to live my last sulfur a life. I wish to be with you. I wish to enjoy each minute lead together. I love you and I think you understand what that word means for me.

Letter 84

[No Subject] December 12

Hello My Love and My Sun!!!

I so like to receive your letters. It is the most beautiful moment for a day when I receive your letters. And for you? You are glad to my letters too?

How you today? What do you do? How you entertain yourself when you are free? You think of me? I do not cease to think of you and I have new dreams of us. I so want all our dreams became a reality.

This night I represented that we have woken up together and near to mine the pillow laid any more. NEAR TO ME YOU LAID!

I have embraced you have kissed very strong. Then you took a blanket and have pulled off it from us. You gently took me and have started to kiss each centimeter of mine a body has been covered by gentle sweet kisses. You did it so pleasantly. I could not be kept began to kiss you too. I was from above you and continued to kiss your breast your stomach all of you below. To us was so hotly that we have decided to open windows. After that we have laid down on a floor continued sweet embraces and kisses. We laid long then I have offered we go to a shower to be washed up.

You took me on hands and we have gone. There we have spent still some time. We did anything you like but only did not wash. You understand about what I speak? To me was so pleasantly with you!

Then I have made a breakfast for us. I have prepared for you pancakes which the grandmother usually prepares. It very tasty. You have told to me "thanks" and began to lick off honey from my lips which remained after pancakes. And we had a long and sweet kiss…mmmmmmm kiss kiss kiss kiss kiss.

After a breakfast we have gone to walk on street. All people looked at us smiled because they never saw such beautiful pair as we!

Darling I the happiest girl. Thanks you for it! I very much love you. kiss kiss kiss kiss kiss.

Tomorrow I will go to the grandmother. I will tell to her "Hello" from you.

I will look forward your answer.

Your gentle and loving Ivana

Letter 85

[No Subject] December 14

Hello My Love and My Sun!!!

You always in my heart always with me. Your letters help me to be joyful happy. I love you! I miss on you. I understand that you write to me and do not want that I longed or missed you but I can do nothing with myself because my love very big to you and I have no so much words to express my love but I hope that you understand it. I am right?

I know that you love me too want that we were happy with you! I want it too! kiss kiss kisss.

I never will cease to think of you because you have taken away my heart. Only you could make me happy. Thanks you for it! I love you!

My mum and Anna speak to you "Hello". I have told them you speak to them "Hello" too. They were delighted to it. All my friends want that we were together because they see I began to smile have every day good mood because always think of you day and night. I cannot live without you!

I hope that I have not bothered you and you wish to hear words of love from me. I hope for it. It is very pleasant to me to listen to love words too.

You the most gentle and tender man!!!!

I love you!! kiss kiss kiss kiss.

I with impatience will wait for your answer tomorrow.

Your gentle and loving Ivana

Letter 86

[No Subject]   December 15

Hi my darling.

I too love you most on the Earth!!! I constantly think of you my love!!!

I so long wanted to meet such fine person as you. I so wait for our meeting with you my love.

I want to see you beside to feel your affinity till day and night. I want to prepare you for a tasty meal have supper with you. I want to walk together with you under a moonlight. I want to feel your hand on my shoulder.

I probably the dreamer, yes, my love? But these dreams warm my heart and give me good mood.

Please write to me more often my love!!!

Love and kisses!!

Yours Ivana

Letter 87

[No Subject] December 16

Hi my love!!!

How you? At me all good. How weather at you?

Your letters bring to me huge pleasure. I want that we were happy with you!!! It is most important dream in my life!!!

I think that ours two destinies should be together. If the person likes this already huge happiness!!!

I want that we woke up in one bed late one food drink one water!!!

The happiness consists in that two loving hearts were together!!!

I LOVE YOU!!!!!!

I WANT YOU!!!!!!

I ADORE YOU!!!!!!

I NEED YOU MY LOVE!!!!!!!

Yours Ivana!!

Letter 88

[No Subject]   December 18

Hi my love!!!

How you? How weather at you? Weather at us very bad!!! There is a cold rain and the strong cold wind blows!!!

I so dream that we go with you for a hand keeping on park!!!

I, likely, as the small little girl!!! But I simply love you my love!!! I think of our first meeting with you!!! I think that it will be simply magnificent!!! I wait dream of it my charm!!!

Each minute when I think of you I roar!!!

I very much would like to embrace you feel heat of your hands all over a body!!! I want that you have embraced me have kissed!!! And when it happen I to a glow at you on a shoulder shall tell to you that I LOVE YOU!!! And I shall embrace you very strongly!!! And we shall dance all night!!!

You would like it, my Prince?

Letter 89

[No Subject]   December 18

My darling how you?

I hope at you all is good. I very strong on you I miss. I love you. This feeling does not allow me to fall asleep easy at night. Darling I very much wish to be in your gentle embraces. I so want it.

So it is a pity to me that we cannot be together. Destiny to me is no fair. Why two loving particles are on different ends of the ground.

My darling I again have a job. I spend time for work. I cannot sit houses and that do. It will be a shame to me before my mum if I shall sit without work. I was fixed up for a job now again. Me any more have not taken for work in hospital because all places have been already borrowed by other people.

Now I work at school as the cleaner. My darling it is necessary for me that to earn for what to buy meal and clothes. You understand that I cannot ask all it my mum. To me work now as the cleaner at school.

I hope that is fast our life to be adjusted and we shall find a way to be together. We shall be happy together.

I shall do all for our love. Only that will know the price of the true love who all will be tested. I think when we shall be tested all this and barrier we shall be the happiest pair in this world.

I love you my Prince.

Letter 90

[No Subject]   December 20

Hello My Love and My Sun!

How you today? I very much love you and miss. For me it is very pleasant to receive your letters and now I have a smile. Thanks you!

How you begin weekend? You have many smiles? I hope, what yes, therefore I do not want that you longed.

I so wish to kiss your smile. And then you will kiss my smile. What do you think? You have what dreams?

Today the pleasant dream dreamt me. I was on a beautiful glade where grew only beautiful flowers. I do not remember as it is called. I very much liked to be there.

I tried to find you among these colours but could not find you. I thought that I will come today in the Internet of café and cannot see your letter but you have written to me and I glad that thought incorrectly.

I so miss on you at night. And you? You think of me at night?

I know that you have similar dreams. We have love which

has reciprocity this most important thing!! You agree with me?

We have still beautiful weather. All conditions to walk but it is a pity to me that we cannot walk together. We can look only at stars together try to see there reflection of our eyes. You agree with me? You look at stars?

I so love you and wish to be with you to carry out all our dreams.

I LOVE YOU!!! I WANT YOU!!! WE WILL BE THE HAPPIEST PAIR ON LIGHT!!!!!!

THANKS YOU FOR LOVE AND TENDERNESS WHICH YOU GIVE ME.

Tomorrow I will go to the grandmother again. I will tell to her "Hello" from you. She will be again glad to hear it.

Your gentle and loving Ivana

Letter 91

[No Subject] December 22

Hello My Love and My Sun!!!

How you today? You missed? I very much missed on to you also looked forward that moment when I can come in Internet of café and see your letter. Thanks you for care and tenderness which you give me.

All time while I was at the grandmother I thought only of you. We again talked to mum and the grandmother about us. They speak to you "Hello" and wish pleasant weekend but weekend has already ended but all the same wished to transfer you it from them. They always good opinion on you and wish us a happy life together. I have told them you speak to them "Hello" too and they so were delighted to it.

I so love you and not want that we divided by the big ocean which I cannot cross or jump over. Sometimes I so want that to me have given a boat that I had possibility to be with you could row to you myself but then to me it becomes sad that I cannot make it. I no know how to row such distance. To me so it is a pity.

I love you and wish to be with you. I want that you knew it!!! I spoke to you about it earlier but I can repeat it infinitely also I will not get tired to repeat it. You understand me?

To me not is suffered to embrace you kiss hold you for hands to feel your smell. It will make me the happiest girl in the world.

My grandmother speaks to me that I became more joyful in a life and have more good mood. Thanks you for it!

Today we have again beautiful weather. It is pleasant to me to go on to street but would be 100 times more pleasant and more beautiful with you.

I so love you!

I will look forward your answer tomorrow.

Your gentle and loving Ivana

Letter 92

[No Subject] December 22

Hello my darling.

Today I very glad to see your letter.

I very much want to wake up in the morning and to see beside you. I would not like to wake up in the morning because I know that you are not present close.

My darling I hope that Our dreams will come true and we shall be happy.

I think the true love can overcome barrier. We consult with barrier and by that we shall prove the love the friend the friend.

Tenderly say to you tenderly I love you.

For me the most important it to be with you. Dear I not have more from a life it is not necessary except for you. I want to divide the life with you. I wish to belong favourite to the person.

It is very a pity to me that we cannot be together on Christmas. I very much would like to be with you for New Year. My darling at us in Russia speak that as you will meet

New Year so him and you will lead. I very much wish to lead New Year with you. I so hope holidays all our dreams will be executed.

I love you.

Yours for a century Ivana

Letter 93

[No Subject] December 24

Hello my darling!

I very much miss on you. I very strongly wish to be with you.

My darling I am tired to wait our meeting I require your love.

My darling for me the most important it you I hope we fast can be together. For me it is very important to meet you. I love you and it is very difficult to me to live without you to me it is very difficult without your love. I very much hope that we can soon enjoy happy time together. I shall be the happiest girl on a planet when I shall have an opportunity to look in your eyes instead of in the monitor of a computer.

I wish to hear words of love from you that you would speak me looking on me. My darling I wish to present you all love which I protected for you.

I shall present all of you the most sweet kisses.

I only for you. Who is necessary to me except for you. I love you. I am ready on all for our love and for the sake of our happiness.

You are very necessary to me.

Your love Ivana

Letter 94

[No Subject] December 25

Hello my darling!

My dear I hope that we shall find a way to meet. I very much would like to be with you on big Holidays which it will be fast. I hope that on New Year's holidays all our dreams will be executed as in fairy tales. I very much like to celebrate New Year.

Usually I meet New Year in a circle of family behind celebratory table. In New Year we gather at my grandmother prepare different tasty pies and salads.

The last New Year to my grandmother together with me and my mum there has gone my girlfriend Anna. The grandmother very much respects with my girlfriend. I heard that in your country the big holiday Christmas. You celebrate him on December 25th? In my country Christmas meets 7 January only after New Year.

My darling you have celebratory mood? At us on work have already put a small fir tree and have dressed up Her. Likely at my grandmother with the grandfather already the fir tree too is established.

My darling as you meet your holidays.

Letter 95

[No Subject]   December 26

Hello My LOVE and My Sun!

Yours the letter makes me the happiest my heart becomes hot and more passionate. Say you we are vibrating to something beyond us! I say it love!

I very much love you!

Merry Christmas I wish you happy Christmas. That all your dreams would be executed.

Last night I looked film "Titanik". It very beautiful film. You agree with me? I could look this film many times because this film very romantic and very sad in same time. Acquaintance Jack and Rose is similar to our acquaintance. You agree with me? I also as well as Jack have casually got there where there was you and has decided to write to you. Jack in film gets on the ship casually too. Then he gets acquainted with beautiful Rose also as well as I get acquainted with you! And they start to communicate and learn each other more. We communicated and learned each other until have grown fond each other too.

I am grateful to you that you have presented me happiness and love which have made me the happiest girl in the world!!!! kiss kisss I love you!!! I would like that we had sex as well as Jack and Rose. It would be passionately and gently. We could make it too.

I never shall never forget that you have not left me and continued to write to me knowing that between us big cold ocean but this ocean not can make cold two hearts because these hearts love the friend the friend also burn fire and nothing can extinguish this fire!!!!!!!!!!! You agree with me?

I dream of you at night and represent that you beside with me gently caress me.

I do not wish to speak about end of film "Titanik" because it very sad.

We shall have a long joint life because we love each other!!! It the strongest love in world which we have with you!

You force my heart to fight more strongly my blood to begin to boil. You can do it. I never met such the man as you!

I LOVE YOU and I SHALL ALWAYS LOVE YOU!!!!! I NEVER SHALL LEAVE YOU!!!! YOU MY LOVE AND MY BIG HAPPINESS!!!!!!!!!!!!!

I WITH IMPATIENCE SHALL WAIT FOR YOUR ANSWER.

YOUR GENTLE AND LOVING Ivana

Letter 96

[No Subject] December 27

Hello my gentle and loving Prince!

I very much love you and miss on you!!!

Today at night the terrible dream has dreamed me. I have woken up and cried. I at all no know how to you about it to tell.

To me has dreamed that I have come in the Internet of café also has not received your letter then have come on following day again has not received your letter then has passed some days weeks and have not seen more your letters. To me it became very terrible that I can to lose you.

And today when I went to the Internet of café I was afraid that you will not write to me and it will be as about volume a terrible dream. And when I has seen your letter now I very much was delighted!! Thanks you big that you continue to write to me and do not leave me!!! I very much am afraid to lose you because I madly love you also cannot live without you!!! This night I was convinced that I very much VERY STRONGLY LOVE YOU AND WISH TO BE WITH YOU!!!

I hope that you understand my feelings. I love you mine

Heart only for you! I shall give nobody you!!!! And me not painfully to cry that is love. Your words in letters so firing my blood.

I continue to repeat to myself that we shall be together. YOU to me is necessary!!! Certainly if not you I would not meet a wind from your far country.

Please I very much ask you that you did not leave me never!!!!! We shall be together forever??? Answer me this question please.

I love you and I very much am afraid, me terribly...

I with impatience shall wait for your answer.

Your gentle and loving Ivana

Letter 97

[No Subject]   December 28

Hello my darling!!

I love you. Your letters always do mine mood cheerful. I with the great pleasure read your letters.

My darling is a pity we cannot embrace each other on New Year as we awake to meet New Year.

Me will not suffice very much without being beside you. My darling speak that thought desire in a New Year's eve are executed. I shall think that we would meet and were together on always. My darling very much does not suffice me without you.

I very much wish to feel heat of your body your gentle kisses. I wish to get accustomed to your body and to conceal in your embraces.

Darling I very much miss on you. I very strongly hope that on 1 February shall fly in volume the plane which will bring me to you. I with impatience wait for that moment when we shall run each other on a meeting.

I live only these dreams. These dreams help to not lose to me hope. I trust in that we shall be together. I love you.

Letter 98

[No Subject]   December 29

Hello My Love and My Sun!

Thanks you for the answer. I very glad to receive it. You always so please me and I with impatience want in the Internet of café to read your letter kiss kiss.

In your house the car with the drunk student has driven???

I thought that the cold and winter will leave and becomes warm but when have woken up in the street there was no sun. There was a grey sky a few snow.

It is inconvenient to go when in the street ice. It because all water which was in the street became ice. Therefore it is necessary to go cautiously. But for children any weather as pleasure because they love both water snow and ice.

It has cheered me up when I have seen joyful children. But it seems to me that such weather is romantic on morning. You agree with me?

It is possible to prepare hot coffee to rise in a window to look that happens in the street. During this moment you could embrace me behind for a waist. Your hands could go on my stomach or anywhere.

You know that each person has special points on a body which do the person very hot. These points are hardly below a stomach and on a back. If you could touch me there would be very pleasant also would become hot.

mmmm…

As soon as I start to think of it I already become hot. You understand me? I hope that we can have a lot of time to investigate our bodies and to find there such special points. What you think of it? kiss kiss.

I kiss each centimetre of your body give much pleasure how many never had earlier.

I so love you! I miss on you and wish to be in your embraces!!!! And you? I hope that you will have many smiles in this afternoon. I love you and miss on you.

Your gentle and loving Ivana

Letter 99

[No Subject] December 30

Hello My Love and My Sun!

I so am glad to see your answer. I always have smiles and happiness when receive it. Thanks you. You do my end of day very joyful.

This night I slept as an angel. I did not wish to wake up because I had such beautiful dream in which were only you and I did not want that this dream came to an end!

We were in a room shined only with light from candles. It was so beautifully and romantically mmmmm…

In room slow and pleasant music played. I never heard such beautiful music. We looked the friend in the face long and enjoyed that moment. I so wanted that it was a reality. I no know during that moment that it only a dream.

You took me for a hand and the second hand have embraced me for a waist. We have started to dance and you have kissed me. During this moment we did not cease to dance but we had very long beautiful kiss. I want that we could repeat it in a reality at once. kiss kiss kiss kisss.

After dance we had a tasty supper with red wine. I do not

drink alcohol but during that moment I have forgotten about all and was ready to do anything you like.

You took me on hands and put on bed. You kissed me so sweet! mmmm and on my body the shiver ran.

I think that in a reality your kisses would be very pleasant and gentle. I am ready to cry now because I feel such happy. I love you! I wish to be with you. I want you!

I very much miss on you day and night.

I look forward to hearing from you with impatience.

Your gentle and loving Ivana

Letter 100

[No Subject]   December 31

Hello My Love and My Sun!

Today again cold day and your letter warms me now. I very glad to receive it. Thanks you that you care of me and give me smiles! I very much love you!

My darling I need for you to be informed that the Internet of café will not work till January, 3rd. My darling today the manager of Internet of café has told that on a holiday of New Year the Internet of café will be closed. To me have told that the Internet of café will not work from December, 31st till January, 2nd. To me have told that I can come on January, 3rd.

I shall miss very strongly under your letter. It is very a pity to me I cannot congratulate you happy New Year during necessary time. My darling I congratulate you on New Year in advance. I love you. I shall miss very strongly and with impatience to wait on January, 3rd.

I no know why but weather began to spoil. It so is sad because I any more do not see birds who sing songs on trees. When in the street the sun beautiful weather also is audible as birds too are glad to such weather. And you? What do you feel in such weather?

I think that it would be very pleasant to us to walk so to hold each other for hands and to talk. This night for me was not so coldly because I was under a blanket and it heated me but if you could be with me at night am assured that I would be more heated from you.

I so love you and want that we were together every night and every day. mmmmmm kiss kiss kiss kiss.

We saw with Anna yesterday and she too does not like such weather. She speaks to you "Hello". In news promise that will be fast again warmly. I hope for it.

For me it would be pleasant if you could heat me now and any weather even a strong cold cannot make me cold. I will be hot about you! You can be convinced of it when we will be together. I love you and I send you my kisses and embraces!! I hope that you will receive it.

I will look forward your answer.

Your gentle and loving Ivana

Letter 101

[No Subject] January 3

Hello my darling!

I very strongly missed on you mine gentle prince. I very glad to read your letter today also very happy to see today your photo. I very much liked new your photo. You are very nice to me!!! I love you. You my gentle prince.

I very much require your love and your caress. I very much did not have all of you holidays. I think that for us every day will be as a holiday when we shall embrace each the other.

I with huge impatience wait for that moment when I can glance your eyes.

My darling I celebrated New Year in circle of family. We with my mum went to the grandmother. By the way my grandmother transfer you “Hello”. She very much wants that in it to year we would be together. My relatives understand all that I very much suffer without you.

I very much wish to be with you. I have thought of desire in a New Year's eve. That we would meet you and have found together our happiness. All these days off I wished to come more likely to the Internet of café and to read your letter.

I now shall wait for tomorrow to come to the Internet of café.

With love yours Ivana

Letter 102

[No Subject] January 4

Hello my gentle prince!

I miss you and think only of you. I would want that we with you were together and all was good for us. I think only of you only you in my heart. I love you.

My darling I very much wish to be near to you. I dream to wake up in the morning once to open the eyes to see beside you. My prince I very much wish to wake up once in the morning from your gentle kiss. My darling I very much miss on you.

My prince is very a pity to me that we do not live in the fantastic world where all easily and simply. I very much wish to be with you but our severe world forces us to live not the close friend to the friend. This world divides our huge love.

I TRUST IN THAT THIS DISTANCE WHICH SHARES US IT TEMPORARILY.

My darling I trust we shall be close. We do not need to mourn in fact we love each other. My darling in this world is easier to live when know that there is a person which loves you. Our love very much helps me.

My prince it is necessary to be pleased that we have met in this huge world.

You do me happy.

I hope that soon we shall together.

I love you.

With love yours Ivana

Letter 103

[No Subject] January 6

Hello my darling.

I know that you awake to care of me when I shall be near to you my darling I as shall care of you. I wish to care of you because I love you. I very strongly love you.

My gentle prince when it is bad to you become to me badly. My prince I glad that at you now all is good.

My darling I shall transmit "Hello" from you Anna and my mum. They will be glad that you pay to them attention.

My darling I all time represent our first meeting. I think: how it will look? What shall we feel? I cannot even express how I shall be happy to see favourite. When I represent our meeting and mentally move there me visits very huge feeling. My darling I understand that I really shall be the happiest girl in the world when we shall be in embraces.

My prince I with impatience wait for that happy minute when we can meet each other. My heart wants to you. I love you. You my unique love in this huge world. I no know as I lived earlier without you.

My darling with you my life has got real sense in a life.

Letter 104

[No Subject]   January 6

Hello My Love and My Love!

I all night long thought of you and waited more likely your answer and now very glad to see your letter.

I so missed on you.

At night I could not fall asleep it seemed to me that time has stopped and was not audible hours. I no know that happens. There was a strange feeling but then I have closed eyes and after a while I could present you as you touch me. I have removed a blanket because when I think of you to me becomes hot.

It is a pity that this feeling passes when I understand that it only dream. I so want that it became a reality and we could feel each other embrace and kiss. mmmmm kiss kiss kiss kiss and you?

In the morning I have woken up with such feeling that you were near to me and have left in the morning. To me was so sadly. In a dream you are very gentle with me and I think that in a reality same as well as in dream.

I so love you!!

I hope what in a reality you will not leave from me in the mornings? I wish to see you in the morning as soon as I will wake up and open eyes. It would be very pleasant and joyful every morning for me will be happy and for you too...I hope.

Now again good and beautiful weather. I wish to walk along the street to take your hand but it is a pity to me that I cannot make it now.

I hope that you will have beautiful day and many smiles.

I love you and I miss on you.

Your gentle and loving Ivana

Letter 105

[No Subject] January 8

Hello My Love and My Sun!

I am very glad to receive your letter. You have once again presented to me a smile and have forced my heart to knock more! I so love you!

My darling yesterday I could not write to you because the Internet of café has been closed. Not who has not warned me that the Internet of café on January, 7th will be closed yesterday at us there was a holiday Christmas and because of it the Internet of café did not work. I yesterday came to the Internet of café but he has been closed. To me it was very sad yesterday. My mum yesterday has left to the grandmother for Christmas and I wished to go to the Internet of café and consequently have remained. I stood hour nearby the Internet of café waited when he will open but he would not open.

My mum has arrived today in the morning. How your new day begins?

I think every morning of you. I dream to wake up and fall asleep together with you! I cannot fall asleep yet I will not present you near to me and I know that when we will fall asleep together we will not have a lot of time for a dream because we will cover each other with kisses and our love. You agree with me? And I know what even after 3 hours of a dream at night I will feel well and I will not require a dream because every night I will be with you and you will be with me! I very much love you and look forward the moment when our dreams can become a reality. And you?

Today we have not so cold weather and will be fast very fast warmly in the street. When made a breakfast today I talked to mum. She asked as you. I have told that you well. Mum has told to you "Hello". She wants that we were happy and had no burning and grief only happiness and love!!! I have told to her thanks and have kissed her on a cheek from us with you. I and my mum we wish you beautiful day and many smiles. I look forward your answer.

I love you and I miss.

Your gentle and loving Ivana

Letter 106

[No Subject]   January 10

Hello My Love and My Sun!

I so am glad to receive your letter. To me it is joyful now. Your letter has very much pleased me. How you?

My darling I would send you my photo that it not has pleased you much. I love you transmit you the most sweet kisses.

KISS KISS KISSS…

Today we have a few solar beams. It so is beautiful when wake up in the morning and can see the sun. You agree with me?

I did not sleep at night yet have not presented that you lay near to me. mmm to me it was very pleasant.

I closed eyes have laid down with bed edge. I have presented that you lay on the right. I did not open an eye because was afraid of you not to see nearby. To me it was very good. We have no more colds and night was not cold. I no know warmly to a room have warmed me or you. I did not take a blanket at this night slept without a blanket. I could not feel your hands but mentally you were near to me.

How you like to sleep? You take a blanket always? How you think we will take a blanket when we will sleep together? I think that was not present because to us will be very much hot when we lay together. The passion hot kisses will not allow to us to be cold. You agree with me? When I think of you and that we will do together I become very hot. mmm And you? I love you! I very much want you!! kiss kiss kiss kiss and you?

My mum speaks to you "Hello" and I have told that you speak to her "Hello" too. I hope that you will have beautiful day and many smiles.

I miss on you.

Your gentle and loving Ivana

Letter 107

[No Subject]   January 10

Hello my darling!

My darling I examined website to hospital. I could not understand there at once. My darling I think that I can find work there. I shall not live at you without work. I equally to find all what not be work. My darling we shall work together to save our family budget.

My darling I very much wish to be close with you. I love you. I shall make all for our general happiness.

To me it very bad without you. I miss on you. My darling is very a pity to me that now I can dream only about a touch to your body. I very much wish to feel your gentle kisses. I hope that soon we shall grant all our secret desires.

My darling I love you. I very strongly miss on yours caress. I think you understand as me hard to live here without my favourite person. I love only you who is necessary to me except for you.

You my far dream. I very strongly hope what be fast we can be together. I live this hope. Without you I not when cannot be happy on the present. You my happiness. I thank destiny that she has presented me you.

Letter 108

[No Subject] January 12

Hello My Love!

Last evening after a supper I drank tea with sweets. It were tasty sweets. I have put half concerts in a mouth and have presented as you could take second half of sweet from my mouth. It seemed to me very romantic beautiful kiss. We would have the most sweet kiss. You agree with me? I hope that you would like it.

I so love you and wish to be together with you that every minute every second we could feel each other. We will be the happiest!!!!

I love you and miss on you.

Your gentle and loving Ivana

Letter 109

[No Subject] January 13

Hello My Love and My Sun!

What you did without me today?

This night I had sweet and gentle dream. How you think what were in this dream? You do not guess? I to you now will tell.

I have woken up early in the morning from a strange feeling as if someone embraces me for a waist. I could not understand but then have opened a blanket and have seen there you. You understand? I could not believe that it the truth.

I did not begin to awake you because wished to look at you in sweet sleep. It was very pleasant to me to look at you. I no know why but I not a pier to tear off a sight. I have bent down to you and have kissed you. You only have turned over on other side. I did not begin to awake you have gone on kitchen to prepare for you coffee.

I have come to a room from coffee and you have woken up. I have told to you "Good morning". You have woken up and you had such reaction as if you did not expect that I will be a close. I had such feeling that you slept too did not guess that I near to you. You understand me? You too could not believe that we together but we have forgotten about that coffee which I have prepared for you began to embrace kiss passionately.

We did it very long then we have gone to a shower and began to have breakfast after a shower. You were very happy I could not remove my eyes from your smile.

Then we have gone on walk to park. In the street there was a beautiful weather. It is surprising because we have spent all the day long in one dream. It happens for one night. How it can be? But it is not important because I already happy that could be with you at least in a dream.

I understand what I will ask a strange question but you had no same dream? You were with me in a dream? It is very interesting to me to learn about it.

I so love you want that we were together not in a dream. I want that we were together in a reality. And you?

I will wait for your answer tomorrow.

Your gentle and loving Ivana

Letter 110

[No Subject]   January 14

Hello My Love and My Sun!

Your letters help me be joyful happy. I love you!

My darling that a photo in a white dress the newest photo.

I miss on you. I understand you do not want that I longed or missed you but I can do nothing with myself because my love very big to you and I have no so much words to express my love but I hope that you understand it. I am right? I know that you love me too and want that we were happy with you! I want it too! kiss kiss ksss.

I never will cease to think of you because you have taken away my heart. Only you can make me happy. Thanks you for it.

My mum and Anna speak to you "Hello". I have told that you speak to them "Hello" too. They were delighted to it.

All my friends want that we were together because they still see I smile have every day good mood because I always think of you day and night. I cannot live without you!

You the most gentle and tender man!!!! I love you!!

I with impatience wait for your answer tomorrow.

Your gentle and loving Ivana

Letter 111

[No Subject]   January 15

Your letters help me to live. With them it is easier to me to carry our separation.

My darling we shall be together on February, 1st? It is very a pity to me that under my pillow there was no today a jewel which price some thousand dollars. I very much wish to be fast in your gentle embraces. I very much do not have your caress your love. To me it more often removed dreams where we together. I cannot live without you. I constantly think of you. My ideas dreams all only about you my love.

Today the dream has dreamed me we were together on a desert island in very cosy hut. You it is sweet slept after we have terminated to make love.

It wanted to bathe and I have gone on coast. I slowly came cool water washed my body. And suddenly I have felt that behind me who that is. I have felt gentle embraces! It were you!

On our naked bodies dim light of the moon I fell looked in your fine eyes they shone. This shine as light of a far beacon was beautiful so much that I should tell not words. We stood on a belt in water looked against each other. On transparent water there was an image ours merged together. I admired your eyes they so are fine. I not when did not see such fine eyes. Such eyes one person the best fine in the world can possess only. And it you my angel!!!!

I so happy have found you. You my ideal! When I wake up on my face a smile I is happy. I very much wish to be only with you.

I send you millions the most sweet and gentle kisses.

With love yours and only yours Ivana

Letter 112

[No Subject]   January 16

Hello My Love and My Sun!

My heart your heart you speak me so sweet.

I no know that to me happens but I cannot fall asleep while I will not present that you not with me. I so love you my heart knocks more strongly and more strongly when I think of you. I love you!

This night I thought of how stars live in the high sky that they think and as they exist. I have thought that if we were stars which always nearby with each other. For them the sky is the big house in which they are and between them is not present the big ocean. They can observe each other. It is a pity that we cannot observe each other with you.

If had the big house as stars and would not have the big ocean between us I would try to go to you to see you embrace you to kiss and if it has happened I more never would release you we would be always together! What do you think of it?

And if we were as a star we would be the brightest stars in the sky because our love would give us such bright fire. You agree with me? I so love you and fire in my heart never will go out while there is you!

Thanks you for your love your tenderness which you have presented to me. You have made me the happy girl.

I send you the kisses and embraces! I hope that it can make to you pleasantly! kiss kiss kiss kiss kiss kiss kiss kiss kiss kiss kiss kiss kiss kiss kiss kiss kiss kiss kiss kiss kiss kiss…

I love you and I look forward your answer.

Your gentle and loving Ivana

Letter 113

[No Subject] January 17

Hello My Love and My Sun!

How you today?

We are the stars in the big house and we have the fire. Thanks you! You warm me the letter. I so love you!!!!

We began to have more snows than yesterday. The nature becomes very beautiful. And how at you weather? At night became colder and consequently want that it came to me in a dream to heat me at night. You try to do it too? You think of that to us it was warm together when in the street a cold wind and a snow? I so want it!

I could not fall asleep while have not presented that you beside with me. My pillow began to have more than embraces from me because I to it more embrace at night. I think of you. I hope that you too do also.

My love the greatest to you. Anybody so does not love in the world as I love you! I know that you have greater love to me too. I very grateful to you for it. Thanks you that you could present me happiness and love. I all life dreamed of this happiness and you and only you could make it. I so love you!!!!

When we shall be together I shall not let out to you from my hands. To you will have to get used to it!! I hope that you will not be against I shall embrace kiss you constantly.

I love you and I look forward to our meeting!

I shall wait for your answer tomorrow.

Your gentle and loving Ivana

Letter 114

[No Subject] January 19

Hello My Love and My Sun!

Forgive me please that I could not write to you yesterday. I thought that I will work and then to have a free time but I have gone to the grandmother and consequently could not write to you. I have told to her "Hello" from you and she speaks you it too wishes you good week many smiles.

I thought that the warmly will soon begin and in the street will be warm but in the street is cold. I no know how will be long cold.

It a pity that we not together now. I so want that you have warmed me your heat tenderness. I would nestle on you and it will not be necessary for me of warm blankets because you will be a number and your heart will so knock that can warm me.

I very much love you! I miss on you. I hope that words in the letter can transfer you my feelings. I very much would wish to lay on your breast now to hold you for a hand. It very much excites my heart. kiss kiss kiss. And you? What do you feel?

I am assured that our nights will the most gentle and

pleasant in our life. We will have joint happiness which we so waited with you. I even did not think earlier that love so heats heart and calms soul. And you? This night I slept so well. I did not wish to wake up because I was with you in a dream. You were such gentle with me your hands went on my body and it was so pleasantly for me. mmmmmmm kiss kiss kiss I hope that you have similar dreams with me. I so love you both I miss on you and I want that we were together as soon as possible. I will miss on you.

Your gentle and loving Ivana

Letter 115

[No Subject]   January 20

Hello My Love and My Sun!

I feel many smiles. You are my life.

You again heat me your letter. I very much was delighted when have seen the letter.

To me was so alone at night. In street there was again a cold. I cannot understand our weather. Several days ago there was a lot of sun and hot in the street. Now again a cold. I have frozen at night. I did not think that will be so coldly. When I slept it seemed to me that in my dream was a cold wind. To me it became cold and there was you and have started to heat me your heat. To me became so pleasantly that I did not wish to let off you.

When I have woken up in a room was cold but I strong embraced a pillow. I have understood why you have come to me to a dream. I have thought of you and have embraced a pillow. I thought that I embrace you.

It is a pity that I cannot do it in a reality. I so wish to be with you now to kiss you embrace at night. I will not let off my embraces!!

I hope that we will not have cold nights as I have it now in loneliness without you. We will have hot passionate nights!! mmmmm I already represent it!

I hope that you have beautiful weather today. I love you and very much miss on you. My mum speaks to you "Hello". I will look forward your answer.

Your gentle and loving Ivana

Letter 116

[No Subject] January 21

Hello My Love and My Sun!

How you today? What did you do as soon as have woken up? I have thought at once of you when have woken up and have thought that you do now. You missed?

My darling I very much wish to fly to you on February, 1st. I love you shall make all for our love and for our happiness. I very much regret that I cannot make for our meeting. Even if I shall not buy to myself meal and not what clothes I shall save up that sum only years through 7-10. When I think it to me it would be desirable to cry. I try to not think of problem but I think of it.

Me it is very bad without you. Today I had beautiful day. I have woken up as I have told have thought of you. I so wished to embrace you and to kiss. Then I would tell "Good morning ". And you? You would like it?

Each time when I have breakfast I wish to prepare for you a breakfast. I so want a happy life for us that we could have many smiles in the mornings together.

I have gone for work at a bus stop there was a young pair they held each other for hands. I want that we had also.

What do you think of it?

On work again thought of you. Only you in my head. I constant with you in thoughts but it is a pity what not a body.

In the street beautiful weather. Many people prefer to walk this evening. And what you prefer? To go by the car or to walk on foot? I love fresh air more. I so want that we had joint walks with you.

And here after work I have come to the Internet of café. I so am glad that you have written me the letter. You have again presented to me happiness and a smile. Thanks you for it!

I so love you and I miss. I will look forward your answer.

Your gentle and loving Ivana

Letter 117

[No Subject] January 22

Hi my dear and beloved!

I had dream last night that you and I were together. In my dream we were on a large fur rug on the floor in front of it. My heart has been totally captured by you! We sat for a while just looking into each other's eyes. We then leaned toward each other shared a long passionate kiss. It seemed as if time were standing still for us. Our bodies came together and we made love for the first time. Afterwards we laid there holding each other professing our love.

When I woke I was very happy you next to me and my heart in my dreams.

I want to have you near.

It was a wonderful dream that will someday come true.

I LOVE YOU MY DEAR!!!!!!!!!!!!!!!!!!!!!!!!!!!

With love and hope Katy

Letter 118

[No Subject] January 23

My darling I wished to subscribe kitten. I wished to name myself a cat. My darling why you carp at it? I no understand that you confuses. To me it is very sick that when I wished to name myself as that on another does to you painfully. My darling I do not understand about what deceit you speak.

You know what girls like to name themselves any names?

Letter 119

[No Subject]   January 24

Hello My Love and My Sun!

I so am glad that you understand it now.

How you has begun weekend? What did you have the interesting? I have woken up and have pulled my feet. Became so pleasantly because the gymnastics help to wake up. You agree with me? You do it too?

I wished to tell "Good morning" but have then understood that you are not present nearby though at night I thought of you tried to present that we together. At me it has almost turned out but I could not receive real sensations when I kissed you.

From the side it likely as so funny to look that I try to kiss you. Before a dream I again took a pillow and embraced it until have fallen asleep. I felt so well that have fallen asleep in your embraces. And you? You think of it as I?

I so love you and wish to be with you!! All my dreams desires only about you! I cannot live without you!! I love you!!! I hope that you understand my feelings. I become joyful always when I can read your letters.

I understand with each new day that you are very necessary to me. Only with you I will be happy. I wish to be with you!! I love you!! What do you think of our feelings? I constantly ask a question when we can be together. I so want that it was already today!!! My heart knocks more strongly and more strongly when I think of you. You are necessary for my life for my heart. You understand my feelings?

Today we have beautiful but cold day. The sun shone in my window when I have woken up today. And you?

My mum speaks to you "Hello".

I love you and I miss on you!

Your gentle and loving Ivana

Letter 120

[No Subject]   January 25

My darling yesterday I with my mum went to the grandmother. I very much missed on you in villages. Today at me good mood because I can read your letter.

I hope that soon we shall together. My darling I very much wish to be in your embraces. I wish to be with favourite. I no wish to live one without love and caress. I wish to feel your hands your gentle kisses.

I hope that on February, 1st I can fly to your embraces. I cannot transfer our separation. Every day for me torture if I cannot be with you. I love you. I very tired to me very much there is no your love.

I cannot feel the happy girl if you are not present close. I want that we would be together on always. I not to whom shall not give you.

You mine I yours. You my most favourite. I not whom so do not love and did not love as you. You for me the most dear in this world. For me there is no not more dearly than you.

Letter 121

[No Subject]   January 26

Hello my darling!

My gentle prince I very much miss on you. I know that to you too it is bad without me. I know that we shall be the happiest pair together. I love you. I very much would wish to make love to you.

I wish to try all in sex! I assured that you very skilled the man and can train me in all.

I would want that we now sat at one table that we would look in the face each other. Then you would approach to me have gently kissed and would call in a room. You would take me on hands then have gently put on a bed began to kiss gently passionately then undress me plant to yourself on knees and we would be carried away with the river of passion and love. We would make love all the night long. At morning we would fall asleep. When we wake up we would be naked. I would rise and have gone to do to you coffee. We send that as though have drunk on a mug of hot café we would continue to be engaged in sex!

I very much want it. I wish to feel your breath each yours touches. I love you my hot prince! My gentle prince I very much hope that already soon all our dreams can be carried out and we shall enjoy each minute lead together.

I love you, yours Ivana

Letter 122

[No Subject]   January 28

I very glad to receive your fine letter. Your letters bring to me a lot of happiness and smiles! I very much miss on you my gentle prince. I very much wish to be in your gentle embraces. All my ideas heart are borrowed only by you and ideas on you. I very much want to you. I wish to feel all your caress love tenderness. I do not have not enough your heat.

To me it is very bad without you! I very strongly wish to be with you!!!! I would want that our lips merged in hot passionate kisses. I would want that you passionately breathed spoke me that you love me. I would want that you caressed language lips my ears.

I dream to cover your fine body with kisses every day! I very much like your dreams would give all that they were executed. I very strongly wish to be necessary with you to me only you your love. My heart soul and a body all asks to you! I very strongly love you. I all would give what now to be with you. About my love I very much like your dreams. I very much would want that they were executed as soon as possible! Your dreams are fine!!!

We shall be the happiest pair on the ground when we shall be together. Our love every day grows stronger. Our love is strong and together we can overcome all on our way. The love this feeling which allows two loving people to do miracles.

We in Russia have such saying "Separation for love as a wind for fire, small extinguishes and big is inflated". By me think this very correct phrase. He reflects in itself very correct sense. Our love is strong also separation for us only more to fall in love us in each other. I cannot live apart from you any more! My heart cries from a pain. This pain will go out only when we shall be together!!!! I hope that what be fast we can together forever!!!!

I adore you my Sun! You for me as a ray of light in the dark sky. You shine only for me you shine to me a way fortunately with you!!!! I cannot live without your love caress!!!! I very strongly want to you my angel. You my second half!!!!

I want to you. I wish you to see to embrace to kiss! I wish to give you every day all love!!!!

I with impatience shall wait for your following letter!

I LOVE YOU!!!!!

I send you millions air kisses they will warm you while I cannot warm you the kisses and the body.

Letter 123

[No Subject]   January 29

Hello my darling!

It is very a pity to me that to us will have to transfer date of my start for next month. I have received my visa of all for 6 months. We will have very few time together. I have received my visa already on November, 14th. My visa is given out to me only for 6 months. My passport for travel abroad operates 5 years and the visa only 6 months.

My darling is very a pity to me that we cannot think up soon. I very much want more likely in your gentle embraces. I wish to embrace you not release you from the embraces. I very strongly love you. I wish to be engaged with you love. I madly wish to feel heat of your body hear palpation of your heart.

My darling I wish to present you the most sweet kisses. I very tired to wait for our meeting but am ready to wait it eternally because I do not love except for you not whom. You are necessary to me only.

My prince I am born for you. It is our destiny to be together.

To me very painfully to experience our separation. My

darling I miss on your caress on your gentle embraces. I hope that soon everything will change also we shall enjoy our love.

I know that is fast we shall be happy together.

Letter 124

[No Subject]   January 30

Hello My Love and My Sun!

How you today? I thought what you do and whether you think of me. I went to the Internet of café and hoped that you will write to me and now glad to see your letter and read it.

What you do now? You sleep or work? You walk or sit at home? You write me the letter or simply you think of me? That you would not do I will be glad for you but only do not long. It is not necessary to do it! It is not necessary to be sad only because between us the big distance. I know that it prevents us to be together but we nearby with each other we nearby we think at night about each other because we love each other.

I do not cease to embrace a pillow. It does me more joyfully. I will sometime embrace you and you will embrace me too. I so want it.

Today beautiful weather again. It very much pleases me. In the street snow becomes more and more. It forces me to walk longer along the street after I will write you the letter. I represent that you receive my letter and smile. I rejoice because of it to me it is very good on soul because I know that you do not long during this moment and think of me.

Children will soon go for a drive from mountains on sledge. It is very interesting to observe of this event because I went for a drive from mountain in the winter but it was in the past but you know sometimes I would like to become the child and to play in childish pranks. And you?

I very much love you so want that you held my hand now and we long talked. It so is romantic when in the sky the full moon stars shine only for us. I want that such moment has come as soon as possible because I love you and very much wish to be with you!

I will look forward your answer.

Your gentle and loving Ivana

Letter 125

[No Subject]   January 31

Hello My Love and My Sun!

How you? I very much love you so miss on you. I no know that to me happens but I with each your letter become happier! I so am happy! Thanks you for it! I become joyful already when I see your letter! I hope that you also are happy as well as I!

This morning have seen a beautiful picture behind a window. As soon as have opened curtains behind a window snow fell. It was a little but very beautiful! Then I have laid down again in a bed also did nothing but needed to go for work.

I have prepared tea and sandwiches. I so wished to make it for you too. It is a pity that we not together now. We would have the most sweet breakfasts with you. What do you think of it?

Children always rejoice when not to street snow and today not an exception falls. Children so are glad to it as well as I rejoiced to snow earlier.

I return to massage at hospital with patients. With everyone we wait doctors let off people home. All thank doctors and me too. I glad for them. I advise to all that they took vitamins to be steadier against illness.

When we will be together I will care of you and you should not stir to me in it. You understand me? I will be very attentive to your health!

I love you will be always with you and will try that you had no reasons to be ill.

I so miss on you. I always think of you. I want that we had long nights and beautiful mornings gentle days when we will carry out all our dreams in a reality. I so want it! kiss kiss kisss I love you. Want that you knew it never forgot!!!! You my happiness and my love!! I grateful to you that you have presented to me such beautiful feeling!!!! I love you!!!

I will miss on you and to wait for your letter.

Your gentle and loving Ivana

Letter 126

[No Subject] February 1

Hello My Love and My Sun!

I so glad you have written to me today. I missed on you! I cannot present to myself as I will be happy when we can be together when I can hold you for a hand kiss you!!!

Today I had beautiful morning. I have noticed that recently I have beautiful dreams wake up to in the morning. And you? It all because I have grown fond of you and I understand how it is good to have love. I so love you!

Now my life began to have the big sense to be with you to have a happy and joyful life with you! I very much want that our dreams became a reality soon. And you? Every morning at us will begin with a smile a sweet kiss. You agree with me? I very much want that it has soon happened to us.

My mum says that it is very pleasant to her to look at me because I have big love and the big love is you! Mum speaks to you "Hello". She wishes for us love and pleasure!!!!! I have told to her thanks have kissed her have told to her "Hello" from you.

We talked how you should get used to Russian food but I

think that it will be pleasant accustoming for you my love!! You will agree with me when will try it. I assured of it. But I could prepare your food if you have learnt me to prepare it. I quickly study to prepare new dishes it no problems for me. You understand me? I so want that we had a meeting and a happy life together more likely!!!!

I very much love you!!!! I send you hot sweet kisses. I hope that it will be pleasant to you to receive it.

Your gentle and loving Ivana

Letter 127

[No Subject]   February 1

Hello My Love and My Sun!

I very much missed on you and looked forward your answer. And you? I so love you!!!!!!!! kiss kiss kiss. I hope that you understand my feelings.

Yes I like to feed with bread ducks. We shall do together when arrive.

I yesterday went to a shower. To me it was very pleasant that water flew down on me and it did to me some massage but I think that it not so is beautiful. If you could be with me in a shower to me would be very pleasant would feel that I am hot. To me it will be hot with you in any weather. Our hearts will knock very strongly. You agree with me?

I will try to do for you pleasant things every day that you felt the happiest. I already feel happy because I love you and love is the most beautiful feeling which the person can feel in heart. My heart big and it for you!!! My life and washing heart only for you!!!

I hope that you understand my feelings. I wish to embrace you to kiss you that you had every day smiles happiness. I love you!!!!! I send you my kisses embraces and hope that you will receive from it the big pleasure!! kiss kiss kiss kiss kiss kiss kiss kiss kiss kiss kiss kiss kiss kiss kiss kiss kiss kiss kiss kiss kiss kiss kiss kiss.

I hope that you have beautiful day and smiles.

I love you and look forward your answer.

Your gentle and loving Ivana

Letter 128

[No Subject] February 3

Hello my darling!

I very strongly miss on you. My darling today on my work was not loaded day. I today worked not much. Patients was not it is a lot of.

I today sat at a window looked at street. I dreamed of us. About our joint happiness. I very much wish to be in your embraces. My darling me very painfully to transfer our separation. I dream only about that time when we shall be together.

The last night I long could not fall asleep. I thought of you. I thought that you are engaged. Thought of that as you without me. I thought of whether you think about to me during this moment. I think of us much.

At me from a head not there are ideas on our meetings. It is very a pity to me that I cannot to move in time. I so want that today would be day of our meeting and we were already together. My darling I very strongly hope that that time will soon come also we shall be together. I love you.

Yours, Ivana

Letter 129

[No Subject]   February 4

Hello My Love and My Sun!

I very glad to receive your letter enjoy each your word. I so love you miss on you every day every night. kiss kiss kiss.

Today had beautiful day. I hope you had today red cheeks because since the morning I thought of you and if I had such possibility I necessarily would kiss you have embraced because I was happy for all life. I need to be only with you to feel you your breath a touch to my body. It so excites me! And you?

All my dreams all my desires only about us you! You have helped me to understand that the life is very fine when have love and though this love very far from me it does me very happy gives me happiness smiles. Thanks you for it! I very grateful to you want that you were happy also as well as I!!! I love you! And I will not get tired to repeat it!!! I LOVE YOU! I LOVE YOU! I LOVE YOU! I LOVE YOU! I LOVE YOU! I LOVE YOU! I LOVE YOU! I LOVE YOU! I LOVE YOU! I LOVE YOU! I LOVE YOU! I LOVE YOU!

You my love my happiness!!! And in spite of the fact it is far every night we are together and to me is sad when in the morning I wake up do not see you nearby but me there was so pleasantly to think that you near to me. mmmmm kiss kiss kisss…

I look forward your answer.

Your gentle and loving Ivana

Letter 130

[No Subject]   February 5

Hello My Love and My Pleasure!

How you today? What did you do? You thought of me? I very much missed on you thought every minute. kiss kiss kiss.

Today we again have snow!!!!! I so am glad to it! All nature as though has changed on eyes! I very much love when such weather in street.

I leave on street and can walk very long but it is a pity to me that we not together now because this walk would be much more pleasant with you than without you!

I hope that we can walk together hold each other for hands. I so want it! And you?

In the evening in places where lanterns do not burn is very light too because snow helps it. I so love when such weather. To me it becomes very joyful.

I remember. When we rushed snow in the childhood it caused in nanosecond a lot of laughter and pleasures but the childhood has passed and now I recollect it with a smile. You often recollect the childhood?

My mum says that I was earlier very careful the child and not as my friends. They liked to roll in snow yet do not become absolutely wet but I so did not do. I always shook off snow from my clothes and there was home a dry. Mum praised me for it. It was valid very interestingly in the childhood. Many my friends have left to study and work in other cities but I remained with Anna and do not regret about it because I could get acquainted with you.

I very much love you wish to be with you embrace you never to let off from my embraces.

I with impatience wait for your letter tomorrow.

Your gentle and loving Ivana

Letter 131

[No Subject] February 6

Hello My Love and My Sun!

Why you today have not written to me? I very much miss on you. How there has passed your day today? What did you do? You thought of me? I know that thought. We feel each other on distance.

Sometimes my cheeks become red and mum speaks to me that any person thinks of you. I say at once to mum that you thinks of me. Mum smiles says that you too should redden. It is interesting to me to learn. You redden too as well as I?

We long talked to mum while made a supper. She speaks to you "Hello".

Today I passed by park. There already it is a lot of snow and children play with it. I so like to look at children. And you?

I have thought that we could play with children laugh rejoice lives. What you think of it? With you I wish to feel the child too near to you. Because you for me the strongest and courageous man near to whom I will feel confidently at same time easy.

I so wish you to embrace now. mmmmmm kiss kiss kiss kiss kisss I very much love you I miss but think of a day when we will be together and we can carry out all our dreams.

I LOVE YOU!!!!!!!! KISS KISS KISS KISS KISS!

I with impatience wait for your answer tomorrow!

Your gentle and loving Ivana

Letter 132

[No Subject]   February 8

Hello My Love and My Sun!

I glad to each your word which you write me it heats my heart and my soul. Thanks you for these it! I very much love you! How has begun your day today? It was with a smile? I think what yes because you could feel that I think to you. You felt it?

As soon as I wake up I start to think of you. mmmm it is such beautiful dreams when we wake up together and we can feel a touch to each other. You kiss me on a cheek then it turns to gentle beautiful kiss. Then we go on kitchen there overcome by passion which forces us to make love on kitchen. I no know how it happens but I think that you can make to me very pleasantly. I will enjoy you. I want it. I very much want it. And you? What could we do still? How you think? I no know so much about it but you can tell and show me it. Yes?

How your weather today? We have only not a weak cold which only reminds of winter and already soon spring. All nature will soon revive and sing. I like to observe of it but it does not deliver me such happiness as you could make it!

I so love you and wish to be with you! mmm kiss kiss kiss!

I will miss on you and with impatience wait for your answer.

Your gentle and loving Ivana

Letter 133

[No Subject]   February 10

Hello my darling!

I very strongly missed on you yesterday. Yesterday I was at my grandmother in villages. My darling me it was very boring without your letter without your warm words.

My darling today at me was a lot of pleasure when I saw your letter. I shall try to find from all forces what not be the sum. I tried to find but now not that it is impossible. I shall try to ask all friends even on not to the big sum. I think it can to us though not many to help.

My darling I very much wish to be in your embraces. We about yours correspond 5 months it much. Not many more months also there will be a floor of year. My darling I learn shall find out how many it will be necessary money if I shall go to you for smaller time. I hope that the sum will be much less. For me very painfully to live an instant without you.

I tomorrow shall start to prolong our visa. It good that the passport for travel abroad is valid 5 years.

My darling you know how I am tired to wait for that minute when our eyes will find each other in the airport.

During this moment I on the top of the world with happiness. Only you can make me happy. My darling I love you. I love you above all. It is necessary for me of that without you.

You for me all.

All this time of correspondence with you I understood every day that you person I searched for all life. I wish to live with you divide our happiness for two. I think we shall be the happiest people on this planet. People do not appreciate the happiness if it gets to them easily. We with you already have overcome much for this time.

We long go to our happiness and I am assured that we shall value very much to ours happiness.

I love you, Ivana

Letter 134

[No Subject]   February 11

Hello my darling!

I very much miss on you my prince. We can change our status for the husband and the wife. My darling I no know how it to make. It is very a pity to me. I would be the happiest girl in the world if we were together. I love you. I very much wish to be the wife. I madly wish to be near with you.

My darling today went to travel agency and have found out how many it will be necessary to have at myself of money if I shall arrive to you for 2 months. Me have told that for this purpose I need to have 1470 dollars. My darling this money not necessary to spend they are necessary for showing only at customs. For 2 months we could change our status for the groom and the bride. My darling I think what to change the status it possible only when we shall be together.

My darling I hope that soon we shall create the family. I love you. I very much do not have your love. Now we can be together only in dreams. Today I dreamt as we spend our evening together. I did not wish to wake up. My darling I wished to remain in a dream because in him we together and are happy.

You my happiness.

Now only your letters give pleasure to my heart. I live your letters. I scoop from them force hope for our happy future.

For all time Ivana K

Letter 135

[No Subject] February 12

Hello my prince.

How are you? My darling I very strongly miss on you.

My lovely prince I wish to be with you every minute the life. I love you. I ready to tell about this to all planet. All my close people wish our of good luck. My grandmother very much wants that we with you would be together. She to pray for our happiness. My darling I too ask the god that we would meet more likely.

I very much hope that all is fast and we shall make for our meeting. My darling I very much wish to carry out all our dreams. I madly wish to be with you near. I ready to live with you all life.

You are very necessary to me. I love you all heart. You are very necessary to me. I require in yours. I want that you would be always in my life want that we were together forever. You my prince whom I searched for all life.

Letter 136

[No Subject]   February 13

Hello my darling.

I very much wish to appear more likely in your gentle embraces. I very much miss on you. My prince I hope that already soon all will occur about what we so long dream.

I shall take with myself birth control pills. My darling I dream every night when we shall be together. I very much wish to give you the gentle kisses all everywhere.

My darling I try to find still what not be the sum but now I am not insolent more in it of success.

I wait for our meeting as a falcon of summer. It is difficult to me to live in this world without your love. It is difficult to me to breathe without you. My lovely you weight sense in my life. I very much wish to be always near with you. I shall hope that we shall consult with all troubles and we shall be happy together on always.

My darling no know where to me to find 1470 dollars, for us it almost 50,000 roubles. In mine town average wages of 5,000 roubles. My darling I at all do not represent who can help me here.

I very much wish hope that something can be thought up.

I love you, Ivana

Letter 137

[No Subject]   February 13

Hello My Love!

How you today? I glad to receive your letter again. Thanks you for that pleasure. I so love you!

What did you do today? How you slept? You thought of me in a dream? I so want you could arrive to me at night when sleep in my dreams. My pillow turns into you every night. I hope that it to happen soon. To me happens sadly sometimes when come from work understand that you very far cannot ask me as my work whether has got tired on work as wish to prepare for you as soon as come from work. What do you think of it?

I think the happiness consists in it and for me very much. That after a tasty supper you could embrace me and cinemas could look then make love. I so want you! What to me to make to help our dreams to be carried out? I so want that at me wings that could arrive to you have grown. And you? You would be glad if I could knock in your window when I would arrive?

I so love you. My feelings very strong to you but it is a pity to me that with my feelings at me wings cannot grow. You understand that I wish to tell? I will make everything that you were happy in this life. kiss kiss but for this purpose we should be together. As soon as it to happen you and I will be the happiest!!! I love you! kiss kiss kiss kiss kiss kiss kiss kiss kiss kiss kiss kiss kiss kiss kiss kiss kiss kiss kiss kiss kiss kiss kiss kiss kiss kiss kiss kiss kiss kiss kiss kiss kiss kiss kiss kiss kiss!!

I think that you have similar dreams of me. I right? So it is pleasant to me to receive beautiful words from you. You the most gentle and romantic in the world!!

I grateful to you for it!! I love you!!!

Your gentle and loving Ivana

Letter 138

[No Subject] February 16

Hello my darling.

I very strongly miss on you. My grandmother and the grandfather speak you “Hello”. My darling my grandmother from the bottom of the heart wishes us happiness she very much wants that we would be together.

I wish to congratulate you on the Valentine's day. At us in Russia it holiday of all enamoured. It is ours with you a holiday.

I so wish to present you now the kiss. It is sad to me that we now not together. I very much wish to be near with you. My darling I very much want that we would find the happiness. I hope soon we shall carry out all our dreams and desires love each other whole nights. I very much wish to spend with you hot nights. I very much wish to be heated by your heat. Be assured I will heat all of you.

I madly miss you.

I perish without your love to edge of a planet.

I believe not that on this holiday we not together.

Letter 139

[No Subject]   February 17

Hello my darling.

My prince I with impatience wait for our meeting. I hope that all is already fast our dreams as in a fairy tale will be executed and we shall be always happy on.

I love you. My darling I so wish to be always close with you. You mine I yours.

I do not wish to live in this world without you. I wish to be always near with you. I wish to spend all the night long in your embraces. I hope that already soon we shall embrace each other.

Yours and only yours Ivana

Letter 140

[No Subject]   February 18

We had beautiful night today. Weather was not so cold in street there was a pleasant wind. I did not wish to sleep. I left on street to stay there. I did not go far from the house. Is simple to me so it would be desirable to take a breath of fresh air. I left and began to think of what nights will be had by us with you. What do you think of it? I think that we will not sleep. I think that we will know the hottest of nights each and every.

Certainly the dream is very important for the person but in me so it a lot of love to you and passion that I cannot fall asleep if near to me you lay!

I so love you!!!! kiss kiss kiss kiss thanks you for your love and tenderness that you give to me. I wish to have night without a dream with you somewhat quicker. It was strange but I almost did not wish to sleep till the morning. I constantly thought of you. In the sky there was a beautiful moon. I looked at it and tried to see there reflection of your eyes. You understand me?

I did not sweep up as have passed hours as I was in the street then have decided to go to the house to lay down to sleep because it is necessary for me for work in the morning. As a result slept some hours. I no know that to me have happened but I could not fall asleep long time. My pillow likely is already tired that embraced her because thought of you. I have not noticed as the dream has come.

It was difficult to me to rise in the morning but I have gathered forces have arisen. My day has passed well I was vigorous.

But now my eyes are closed also I should go home to lay down in bed. I will think of you even in a dream.

Still you think I deceive.

It is very a pity.

I with impatience wait for your answer tomorrow.

You can follow Ivana's continuing saga with
updates every day at *www.twitter.com/IRussianBride* and
interpretive videos at *www.youtube.com/IRussianBride*

ABOUT THE AUTHOR

Mark Katzman has published two artists books, *Inon* and *Along the Way*. He has published interviews and articles in Art Papers, Mondo 2000, Internet Underground, Zavtone (Japan), The Review of Contemporary Fiction, among others. He is the editor of the online zine, artzar.com. He lives in Athens, Georgia.

Made in the USA
Columbia, SC
23 May 2023